The Twins of Fairland

The Twins of Fairland

sb white

authorHOUSE®

AuthorHouse™ LLC
1663 Liberty Drive
Bloomington, IN 47403
www.authorhouse.com
Phone: 1-800-839-8640

Published by AuthorHouse   01/30/2014

ISBN: 978-1-4918-5989-6 (sc)
ISBN: 978-1-4918-5990-2 (e)

Library of Congress Control Number: 2014902010

Contents

Part 1
The Rescue

Part 2
The Hidden

Part 3
The Magic

Part 4
The Forgotten

For Zandra

Part 1
The Rescue

Chapter 1

The young woman hid in the thick bushes. She could hear them coming fast—their horses' hooves pounding the trail into a large cloud of swirling dust. Breathing hard, she choked on the dust and put a hand over her mouth to muffle the cough. She had been running since before dawn, when she had made her escape. She froze in place and held her breath; she did not want to make any noise that could give her away. If she was recaptured, she would never survive the torture that awaited her. The raiders were cruel and vicious, with whips ready to tear the flesh off their victims. She had witnessed it countless times. Before a raid, they would streak their faces red to scare the unsuspecting villagers. At the sight of the villagers cowering in fright, the raiders' laughter rang out ruthless and cold, without a hint of compassion for the innocent.

As she hid, she tried to remember where the trail that hugged the river began. If she followed it upstream, she would come to the small valley that had been her childhood home. She recalled happier times with her mother and father in their small home. She stared at her roughened hands, scarred from years of hard labor. She didn't know how long she had been a captive, four or maybe five years. Time was blurred by the fear of beatings and trying to survive on the meager rations the prisoners were fed. Her determination that one day she would escape kept her alive. What had become of her mother and father? It was a nightmare she could not forget: the running, the fighting, the screaming. She could still smell the smoke from the fire that ravaged the village. She had been captured, tied on the back of a horse, and endured a terrifying ride to the desert land below.

She could not believe the warriors had chased her this far with the threat of snow hanging in the air. They only left their desert encampment to hunt game or raid for slaves in the hot summer months. This was the reason she timed her escape when snow covered the far mountain tops. Crouched in the bushes, she continued to wait and worried that it would be dark soon. Not hearing any sounds signaling the return of her captors, she stood up, looked around, and then started to climb the river bank. It was slower to follow the river, but safer. Night would fall soon, and she must find a place that was safe and would protect her from the cold night air.

*   *   *

A bird's loud squawking woke her. At night she had found a small cave along the river bank and crawled in as far as possible. She had been terrified of being found, but must have slept because she had dreamed of home and of her father holding her above his head and spinning around and of her mother baking bread in the stone hearth. It was the most wonderful smell she could think of. Her stomach growled; it had been over a day since she had anything to eat. Her name was Farin. Her mother had chosen the name, but her father had soon shortened it to Rin.

Rin slowly crawled out of the cave, looking around to see what was agitating the birds. Had her captors returned? She stood up and brushed off the dirt that clung to her clothes. She pushed her matted hair from her face and saw the noisy birds circling above the river. Puzzled at their strange behavior, she climbed onto a rock and saw a small stream that joined the river. The stream came from the tall purple mountains, where a cascading waterfall tumbled to the ground. Rin had never gone there with her father when they hunted for summer berries. Once, she asked why, and he replied it was too far and no one could find a way through the mountain's solid wall.

Rin saw a strange object caught in the abundant weeds growing in the river and, holding a tree branch for support, leaned out over the water to get a better look. It was too small for a boat. The top was enclosed, and she could not see what was inside. It was too far for her to reach, so she stepped off the rock to continue on her way when she heard what sounded like a baby's cry. She stopped, was it her imagination? She heard the sound again. She must hurry but could not leave a baby to drown in the river, if it really was a baby. Rin looked around and saw a broken tree branch. Picking it up, she stepped into the river and gasped; the water was frigid. Setting her feet as firmly as possible in the fast-moving river, she reached out with the branch, hoping to snag the small craft. On the third try, the branch caught hold of the top, and she tugged to loosen it from the weeds. Hand over hand, she inched the small craft across the river until she could reach out and grasp it. Firmly holding it, she stepped backward to the river bank.

With the small craft safely on the river bank, Rin carefully untied the rope that held the top closed. She ran her hand over the top, amazed how precisely each piece of wood was cut, making it waterproof. Even more amazing was what was inside. When she opened the top, a baby looked up at her. It looked to be a year old. The baby had bright blue eyes and hair the color of honey.

Rin lifted the baby from the wooden craft; it was a boy. Inside was a red blanket with strange symbols woven into the cloth. Quickly, she wrapped the blanket around the boy and held him close. *What am I going to do*, she worried. She was in danger, with no way to protect herself. Her chance of survival was small in the wild mountain region and even smaller with a baby. Rin sat down to think of a solution and noticed the quiet; the birds had stopped their loud squawking, and the forest around her had become strangely silent. The splash of water in the river was all she heard. A shiver ran down her back. She sat the boy on the grass and quickly broke the wooden craft into small pieces. She threw them into to river and watched the current carry them away, erasing all traces of the craft. Carrying the boy, Rin struggled up the steep river bank as fast as she could, certain that something or someone was watching them.

Chapter 2

Rin placed the freshly washed clothes on the wooden rack to dry. They were worn and patched. She paused to watch the boy playing in the meadow. A smile spread across her lined face; she was proud at how he had grown. He was a healthy and happy boy. His cheerful laughter always warmed her heart. She recalled the day she pulled him from the river. Cradling him in her arms, she struggled up the mountain to find her home and village destroyed. Only remnants of burnt wood and blackened stones were left to identify her past life. Determined to survive, she continued climbing the steep mountain trail. She did not remember how long she walked before men out hunting found her collapsed against a tree with the baby clutched in her arms. They carried her and the child to a small hidden valley, where, nestled against the mountain, lay their village.

Rin was so exhausted from climbing the mountain and carrying the child that it was two days before she regained consciousness. She was in a small room covered with an old quilt. Rin recognized the woman who hurried over to help her sit up. The woman's name was Beth, and she had been a friend of her mother. Rin tried to speak but could not, her throat swollen from lack of water. She swallowed from the cup Beth held to her parched lips and hoarsely asked about her parents. The look on Beth's face told her they did not

sb white

survive that horrible night. Beth held Rin in her arms as she wept tears that, until now, had not been allowed to fall. All hope was gone, and in despair Rin wanted to give up, but the thought of the baby she had rescued gave her the strength to go on.

When Beth asked her son's name, Rin quickly said, "Tre," after her father, Tresen. She had been afraid to reveal the truth about finding the boy and not knowing where he came from. She feared the villagers would send them away. For that reason, she let everyone think Tre's father was one of the captors she had escaped and she still held this secret. Rin found work in the bakery, baking breads as her mother had taught her. It was hard work, but she was able to earn enough to support the two of them. With help from the butcher, she fixed up an abandoned hut at the edge of the village. It leaned to one side and only had one room, but it was cozy and the stone fireplace kept it warm. The two were happy in the old hut.

Rin continued to watch Tre, to make sure he did not wander too far away. She looked at the tall trees surrounding the small meadow where he played and felt they were being watched, but did not see anyone. During the years they lived here, she had become accustomed to this feeling but for some reason did not feel threatened by it. Numerous wild animals roamed the mountain. She knew there were bears and mountain cats, but nothing ever came around their hut or threatened them when they were outside. Others in the village had animals go missing from their pens and complained of hearing wild animals prowling at night, hunting for food, but she had never heard a sound around their small home.

Once, Rin ventured into the woods above the small hut and noticed a large animal's tracks. The tracks were so huge that both of her hands fit into one of them. The animals that roamed the mountains could never leave a print that big. Why this did not scare her, she could not explain. She had never mentioned these strange tracks to anyone. From the time he could talk, Tre would often tell her about his dream of a large bird that would sit outside the window. Rin would assure him it was only a dream and he was safe in his bed.

Tre would soon be close to ten years old. Rin didn't know his exact birthday and had made one up. What mother would not know her only son's birthday? Every year they celebrated the made-up day with a cake to eat and a candle to blow out. Rin knew the day would come when she would have to tell Tre how she found him and show him the blanket she kept hidden, but not today. That evening after Tre was asleep, she took his old blanket out of its hiding place. As she held it she wondered what the strange markings meant. Who was Tre's real family, and what had happened to cause them to abandon him in a stream, hidden in the small wooden craft?

Tre had grown into a boy with amazing skills. He was far advanced over other boys his age. He understood how anything worked just from looking at it and could fix it when he had the necessary tools and parts. Behind the old hut he had an assortment of stuff he said he might need, and the pile grew daily. Rin told him he was like a squirrel stashing nuts in a tree for winter. Rin had been taught to read and write by her mother, and she taught Tre. He read every book she was able to borrow and bring home. She knew that one day he would grow bored in this small hidden village.

Rin ran her hand over the old blanket, wondering if Tre came from the purple mountains. It seemed impossible; he would never have survived a plummet from the top of the waterfall. Her father told her no one could find a way through the mountains because they were too steep to climb and the rock too thick to cut a way through. Yet, someone had been able to get the boy out. It must have been carefully planned because the strange wooden craft would have taken time to build.

Rin looked out the window and noticed a large bird sitting on a tree limb. She stood up and went to the window. The moon was full, and from its light she could tell the bird was an owl. But that was impossible; owls could never be this large. Its huge eyes seemed to be staring at her, penetrating the darkness. She knew the large bird was the source of Tre's dreams. Rin folded the blanket and placed it on the shelf, hiding it away. She lay down on her cot and looked over at her amazing son, once again pondering the question that haunted her. When would she tell him the truth?

Chapter 3

Tre was in the meadow outside the old hut, practicing throwing the large knife given to him by the village butcher. Its wooden handle was worn and nicked from years of use, but to Tre it was his greatest treasure. He often helped in the butcher shop, moving slabs of meat that had been hung outside to allow the blood to drain to the cutting table inside. The butcher taught Tre the correct way to throw the knife at a circle painted on the shop's back door. His aim was getting better, and he hit the target more times than he missed it. The butcher showed him how to change his hold on the knife to defend himself if ever in a close fight. Every able man in the village owned a weapon and kept it close. They did not want to be caught unprepared if the lowland raiders ever found their small hidden valley. Signs of the raiders had been found since the spring thaw, their scouts hunting for villages to raid before summer's end. In the winter months the ice and snow made the climb up the steep mountain too dangerous for their horses, keeping the raiders in the desert below.

For as long as Tre could remember, one of the village men was always on guard, watching the narrow path that led upward into the valley. He heard the stories about the raid on his mother's village and the murder of the grandparents he never knew. His mother, taken captive, had escaped after years of hard labor, carrying her son with her to freedom. Rin was a hero to everyone, her survival and escape a source of pride for all. She never spoke of her capture to Tre, but he had seen the scars on her back from many beatings. He understood why the men were so determined to avoid the horror that befell his mother's village.

Tre practiced every day with the large knife; soon he would take his place with the other men that guarded the village. He would turn twelve next week and be of age to join the protectors. These were the armed men who watched for the raiders. The protectors knew that one day their village would be found and prepared for the raiders' arrival. Tre would only bring water and food for the guards, but at least he would be doing his part. This was important to him; it drove him. He did not want anyone to know the terror that his mother had experienced.

By age twelve, Tre had grown tall and strong and could outrun anyone in the village. He enjoyed racing the other boys. He would let them get ahead and then sprint past them to win. His mother constantly grumbled about having to let the hems out of his pant legs, saying soon he would be wearing men's pants. Tre was now taller than his mother, and she was almost as tall as the men in the village. Tre's eyes remained startling blue in color, and he kept his honey-blond hair tied back. He often wondered why he didn't have his mother's brown hair and eyes or the darker skin and hair of the raiders. His blond hair and blue eyes made him stand out from the other children in the village.

Tre had many friends both young and old. The children always followed him around when he was in the village. His mother would tease him, calling them Tre's "little flock." She said they looked like a flock of birds following the lead bird.

Tre left the grassy meadow and climbed uphill to the tall trees that circled the hut. He was running, twisting, and jumping, pretending he was in a hand-to-hand fight with his knife, which he sharpened and polished daily. He held it high and vowed he would be ready to defend his mother and his village when the time came.

Tre strutted up the hill, holding the knife forward, and made a leaping jump, landing in a fighting crouch like he had been taught. Laughter startled him. Tre froze; he had not seen anyone around the old hut. It was a girl's laughter. He was embarrassed at being spied on, especially by a girl. Tre jumped up, stumbled on a rock, and fell backward. He dropped the knife when he put out his hand to stop himself from tumbling down the hill.

As Tre lay sprawled on the ground, a strange girl stepped from the shadow of the trees and stood looking down at him. She was as tall as Tre and carried a large wooden staff carved with strange markings. She was dressed in a manner he had never seen before. She had wide leather bands tied around her arms above the elbows with markings on them. Brown boots came to her knees with laces that wrapped around and tied at the top. A wide belt circled her waist. Tied around her head was a narrow band that matched the ones on her arms. Long blond braids reached her waist. She had a wide grin, and her piercing blue eyes sparkled.

"He doesn't look like a great warrior, does he, Cerra?" As she spoke, an extremely large mountain cat stepped out of the shadows and stopped beside her. The cat's head came past the girl's waist, and muscles rippled its wide shoulders. Its dense fur was a dark mustard color. Two eyes as black as night watched Tre.

Tre was stunned at the sight of the monstrous beast. His mouth dropped open, and he stopped breathing. It was odd enough to see this girl standing over him dressed so strangely, but the enormous animal beside her was mind-boggling. Tre lay frozen on the ground, unable to move a muscle. He felt like a cornered mouse waiting for the cat to pounce. One bite from those huge teeth would take his head off. One swipe from its gigantic paw would rip him to shreds. This was not a nightmare he would wake up from. He must get away. *Run.* That was all his brain came up with. He was fast; the hut was not that far. Could he make it? *Run, and run fast*, ordered his brain.

Tre crab-walked backward as he gaped at the bizarre pair, who had not moved. When he got a couple of feet away, he jumped up and ran for his life. His arms and legs pumped at max speed as he raced down the hill. He wasn't sure, but he thought he heard her laugh again. Running full speed, he slammed into the old hut's door, almost knocking it down, and fell inside. He quickly kicked the door shut and collapsed on the floor, panting in fear, not believing he was still alive. Finally his breathing quieted. He listened from behind the door and did not hear any sound of pursuit from the eerie pair.

Tre crawled to the window and peeked out. All he saw was the grass blowing in the meadow and in the trees—nothing, just trees. No strange girl. No huge cat creature. Tre could not make sense of what just happened. He knew he hadn't conjured the pair like a magic trick. They were way too scary. As he looked out from the safety of the old hut, a new feeling came over him. He felt ashamed of how he had reacted in fear. He was no protector. He not only ran for his life like a coward, he left his treasured knife behind on the ground.

Chapter 4

The incident with the strange girl and huge cat haunted Tre. He knew for certain they were not alone and the mountain village had been found. The old hut he shared with his mother no longer felt safe. He looked at the wooden walls, bent and cracked by numerous winters. The one window didn't shut tight, and the door barley closed. He was still embarrassed by how he acted when meeting the strange pair. True, he had been startled, first by the girl and then the cat, but that did not justify his cowardly behavior.

All the next day, Tre kept constant watch out the window and did not leave the hut. Rin asked him what was wrong. Why was he acting so strange? Her happy-go-lucky son had been replaced by a jumpy, nervous stranger. Tre answered his mother with a mumbled "nothing," but he knew *nothing* would ever be the same.

The second day passed, and, seeing no sign the two intruders had returned, Tre ventured outside and slowly crept into the meadow. He continually looked around the meadow. All seemed quiet; cautiously he climbed toward the tree line. He wanted his knife, to start practicing seriously from now on. The time for playing childish games had come to an end. Tre looked right and then left as he slowly stepped ahead. He came to the large rock he liked to jump on and stopped. He spotted his knife up ahead. Inspecting the tree line one more time for strange lurking creatures, he saw none, hurried over, and grabbed his treasured knife. Holding it tightly he realized it had remained exactly where he dropped it. The strange girl did not, as he had feared, take it as a trophy to remember when she scared the village idiot, causing him to run for his life. Tre turned to leave and noticed the girl's large wooden staff leaning against the tree where she had stood. She had left it behind. *Was it on purpose?* he wondered.

Tre saw tracks in the soft dirt around the tree and bent down to examine them. He placed his foot beside her boot print. They were the same size. The villagers wore moccasins, which were flexible for climbing the steep mountain slopes. Her boots looked like they had been made for riding, not hiking narrow trails. He was astounded at the large tracks left by the cat. They were huge, but so was the animal. Tre stood up and followed the tracks further into the trees where they disappeared as the ground became dense with wild grass and tree needles.

Tre's skin felt prickly and he shivered. He had been gone longer than he planned and wanted to get back to the hut. He paused by the tall staff and studied it. It had the same symbols carved into it as the girl's head and armbands. Hesitantly Tre bit at his lip. Coming to a decision, he grabbed the staff, squared his shoulders and marched down the hill. He firmly vowed his days of running like a chicken were over.

Back in the hut he stood the staff in the corner, sat down, and stared at it. He knew he would have to tell his mother about the incident. Maybe they should move into the village. The bakery where his mother worked had an empty room above it. The old couple who owned the bakery had said whenever Rin and Tre needed to move, the large room was theirs and had mentioned more than once the old hut looked ready to collapse; the next big wind would blow it over. But Rin and Tre were happy there, until now.

Tre was sitting out front when Rin returned home after the day's bread was baked. She sensed something was bothering him and sat down beside him. When he was upset, she could always calm him, her soothing voice assuring him everything would work out. Through the years her strong arms held comfort for the boy. Rin stood up and said, "Let's go have something to eat, and you can tell me what has upset you. I bet it's a girl." She laughed and held out a warm loaf of bread for him to smell. "It's your favorite, berry and nut."

Tre joined his mother at a small wood table rescued from the rubble pile. They had fixed its broken leg, but the table still leaned to one side. He looked across at her, sighed loudly, and then he said, "I'm not sure if you'll believe me. Wait." He jumped up, retrieved the staff from the corner of the hut where he had place it, and sat back down.

Rin stared at the staff in disbelief and then closed her eyes. She recognized the carved symbols; they matched the ones woven into the old red blanket she kept hidden. At their rescue, the blanket had been covered in mud, and no one had noticed the strange markings. She hid the blanket until it was safe to wash it and had kept it out of sight since then. Rin opened her eyes and pointed to the staff and asked, "Where did you get that?"

Tre finally told his mother the story of the girl and the cat. He didn't stop until he finished with carrying the staff home. He paused and, staring at Rin, said, "We're not safe here. We should move to the bakery." He abruptly leaned back in his chair to catch his breath. During his long narrative he had been tensely leaning forward.

Rin was silent, taking a minute to sort out the details of Tre's harrowing tale. Then she admitted, "I've seen the large cat tracks before. I don't think they're here to do us harm." She did not seem upset, and Tre was confused. He stared at her, trying to understand her calm reaction. "Don't mention this to anyone. I need time to think about it," she firmly said. Rin stood up, took the staff from Tre, and slowly turned it in her hands. "Have you seen markings like this before?" she asked him. Tre shook his head no. "Put this away and don't show it to anyone." She handed the staff back to him. He felt something wasn't right. Why wasn't his mother worried after hearing his scary story?

Tre had to know. "Are these symbols of the lowlanders?" He was worried the village had been found by scouts.

Rin turned to look at him and said, "No. I've never seen these markings before." She had never lied to Tre before.

"Where do you think that girl came from?" Tre asked his mother. "She sort of looked like me." All the children in the village had brown hair and eyes, as did their parents.

Rin turned away and shrugged her shoulders. "It's late; get to bed. The butcher asked if you would be in tomorrow to help." As Rin walked by the window to the cot where she slept, she glanced out, looking for the large bird.

* * *

Meeting the strange girl with the very large cat had changed Tre. Knowing he and his mother weren't alone or safe any longer bothered him, even if Rin did not seem to be worried. He practiced with the large knife every day. He organized the older boys in a team, taking them through daily drills. They decided to call their new team

Little Flock, adopting the name Rin had given them. They practiced hard every day, and each of the boys had a specific skill they worked to improve. They fought against each other, climbed to hiding places, and created defense maneuvers against specific threats.

Tre asked Dellis to be his second in command. Dellis was a year older than Tre and skilled with the crossbow. Tre had grown during the summer and was now taller than Dellis. The two had become good friends, but Tre still kept secret his experience in the trees. Windel enthusiastically joined Little Flock. He was the smallest team member and wore clothes passed down from the older children that hung on his small frame. He was shy and rarely talked, but his smile made it clear he was happy to be a member of the team. In practice he carried an old sword that belonged to his grandfather, but it was so heavy he would mostly drag it behind him. "Maybe he can trip a raider with it," Dellis had joked one day during drills, causing Tre to laugh.

Little Flock totaled twelve boys, and when some of the girls came out to practice, it grew by two or three depending on the girls' willingness to participate. After meeting the strange girl in the trees, Tre decided the village girls should also know how to defend themselves. He knew the strange girl could defend herself with that large staff. But despite Tre's efforts, the girls mainly watched the boys and weren't interested in running and fighting. They would clap excitedly when a Little Flock member hit a target or giggle behind their hands when one of them would miss.

The youngest girl that watched Little Flock practice was named Moon. Her mother gave her that name because there was a full moon the night she was born. Moon had big brown eyes and long flowing hair that hung to her waist. She had lost her mother two winters ago, and Rin had begun to teach her to bake bread. Moon came to the bakery most days, and Rin had grown fond of the young girl. Tre would listen to them chatting away like birds while they baked the breads. Tre teased her by calling her Moon Bird.

Little Flock marched, went on patrols, and rushed to grab their weapons and assemble when the alarm sounded. As the boys grew, so did their skills. Everyone in the village was impressed at Little Flock's progress and Tre's leadership. More than once, Rin had been told, "He's a born leader." She knew the reason driving him was the visit by the girl with the large cat. Neither Rin nor Tre ever mentioned that visit to any one, and the tall carved staff stayed hidden in the corner of the hut.

Tre turned fourteen this month. He was taller than most of the men in the village. Rin was proud of the young man he had become. The boys of Little Flock were dedicated to Tre with such purpose that it baffled Rin. He was their leader, and they would follow him without question. Rin knew it was time to tell Tre about his past. Maybe she had put it off too long, but until now she wasn't sure if he could handle the truth. She vowed to herself there would be no more lies between them.

Chapter 5

Daylight was fading as Rin sat at the old table waiting for Tre to return from the protector's meeting in the village. Little Flock had become an important part of the protectors and had specific duties assigned to guard the village. The first duty of the day was to check the narrow trail for any signs of the raiders. Next, they would scout the entire village, looking for tracks, but the only tracks they had found were from the wild animals that roamed the mountain. Tre made sure all assignments were completed every day before Little Flock began their drills.

Rin had taken the frayed red blanket from its hiding place and held it in her lap. Looking at the strange symbols, she wondered what they meant. She heard Tre's footsteps outside, and when he entered the old hut, he walked over and hugged his mother. Rin asked, "How was the meeting? Have there been any signs of the raiders?"

Tre sat down at the old table, tore off a large piece of bread, and stuffed it in his mouth, mumbling, "No recent signs." He then noticed the blanket Rin was holding and asked, "What's that? It looks old."

Rin looked at her son and said, "I have something to tell you. Maybe I should have told you before now."

She clutched the old red blanket while she told Tre of her escape from the lowlanders. She did not spare him any details, including the cruel way she and the other captives were treated. How, after years of starvation, they would grow sick and die. She had planned her escape at winter's arrival and had patiently worked many long nights to loosen the poles along the back wall of the cage. When the camp went dark after the evening duties were completed, she quietly removed the poles and escaped from the cage where she had been held captive for years. She ran across the desert all night, finally coming to the river trail that led into the mountains. She had stayed close to the river, hiding from the raiders, afraid of being caught and tortured to death.

She told Tre how the noisy birds had awakened her, their constant circling over his small wooden craft, about pulling him from the freezing river, and climbing the mountain only to find her village destroyed. Barely alive, they were found by men out hunting game and were carried to the high mountain village. The rest Tre knew; he had lived in the old hut outside the village ever since.

As Rin told Tre the story, she began to wonder about the noisy birds' part in finding his craft and why the wild animals that roamed the mountain seemed to pose no threat. How did the men find them in time to save them from the freezing weather? In her weakened state, she had wandered far off the trail that led to the village. It was as if the men had been following tracks that led directly to them.

Rin told Tre that she kept his secret because she was worried they would not be allowed to stay in the village. The villagers would be afraid of not knowing where Tre came from and what danger his origins could bring. When Rin finished talking, Tre was stunned. Now he knew why he was so different from the other children in the village. Finally he asked, "Then who am I? Where did I come from? You are not my mother?" He gasped at the thought that Rin was not his mother. That was the hardest part for him to accept.

"Tre, I will always be your mother. Just because I didn't birth you doesn't make any difference." Rin was adamant that he understood he would always be her son no matter what.

Tre took the old blanket from Rin and held it up. "I wonder what these strange markings mean. That girl had them on the clothing she wore and the staff she left behind." Tre looked at the tall carved staff leaning in the corner. He turned to Rin and said, "This is the reason you weren't afraid when I told you about meeting her."

Rin nodded and then shocked Tre further. "That large bird in your dreams—it's not a dream. I've seen it watching the hut since we've lived here." Rin sighed with relief; now Tre knew everything she had kept secret for so long.

Tre shook his head in bewilderment. "I'm not sure if this all makes sense or nothing makes any sense." He stood up and walked outside carrying the tattered red blanked and looked toward the tree line. There was the large bird perched high in a tree, its huge black eyes looking directly at him. Tre stood and stared back at the bird that had invaded his dreams since he could remember. But it wasn't a dream; it had been real. Tre held up the old blanket and yelled, "I know. I know."

Tre spent the next day with Rin helping out around the bakery. He was still coming to terms with everything she had told him the night before. Many thoughts ran through his mind, but the one bothering him the most was where he came from. He must have a family somewhere. And what about the large bird that had watched over him for years?

Tre did not lead Little Flock that day. Dellis took the boys through their drills. Tre had an uncertain feeling, as if he didn't belong in the village any longer. But where did he belong? He cleaned and swept the bakery, allowing Rin to leave early. They walked together in quiet; it was as if neither knew what to say or where to begin. When they reached the hut, Tre saw the girl and the cat waiting at the tree line. He had been expecting them. He told Rin to stay by the hut, and he walked across the small meadow and up the hill. His steps firm, he would not run away this time.

Tre stopped directly in front of the girl. She had grown in the two years since her last visit. She was as tall as he and dressed in the same manner as before. She held a staff identical to the one in the hut. The large cat that had frightened him before stood protectively by her side. "Who are you?" Tre demanded.

The girl grinned at him, her blue eyes taking in his appearance. She laughed and said, "You've grown in two years and are not a scared rabbit anymore."

Tre repeated, louder this time, "Who are you?" He was in no mood to be nice or play her silly games.

The girl put her head back and laughed again and then said, "Your sister. Notice the resemblance?" Tre had noticed the honey hair and blue eyes from her first visit, but now, standing close to her, he could see they shared the same build and facial features. She stared at him and, her voice cynical, said, "We are twins. Oh, and I'm the oldest."

This was another shock; he not only had a sister but a twin sister besides. Tre wasn't sure he liked the idea. "Where are you from?" he asked, not responding to her revelation about being twins. He wasn't ready to accept this girl as part of his missing family. She didn't say a word, but pointed her staff toward the high purple mountains far away.

"Why don't you come inside? It will be more comfortable than standing out here." Tre had not heard

Rin walk up beside him. She introduced them. "My name is Rin, and this is my son Tre." This caused the girl to smirk, and it annoyed him, like she knew everything, and he knew nothing. Granted, this *was* the case, but Tre did not want to admit it. Perhaps it was an inherent brother-sister rivalry that Tre felt toward her.

The girl spoke to the cat, saying, "Cerra, stay and guard." The big cat seemed to understand and answered with a low growl. "Come on," the girl ordered, and she motioned with her staff like she was in charge and Rin and Tre: her followers. Just because she was the older twin didn't mean she could tell him what to do, he thought.

Rin hurried ahead and opened the door to the old hut and motioned toward the table. "Please sit. Would you like something to drink or eat?" she asked.

Tre grumbled to himself. Why was his mother being so nice to this unwelcome visitor? The girl glanced around the inside of the hut, her eyes taking in their meager existence. Tre stiffened from her apparent attitude. He was proud of their small home. He and his mother had turned the old abandoned hut into their special place. He was happy here and wasn't going to let her superior air ruin it for him. She noticed the tall staff standing in the corner. "I see you found your staff. How long did you wait before you were brave enough to go get it?" She laughed and then said, "You sure can run fast. I bet Cerra would have a hard time catching you." Was she trying to irritate him on purpose?

Rin asked the girl, "What is your name? I heard you call the big cat Cerra. And what about the large bird that sits in the trees most nights?"

The girl looked across the table at Rin and said, "I'm called Skylin. The owl's name is Koda, and he is *Tre's* guardian like Cerra is mine. We were given them as gifts when we were born." Why had she had paused like that when she said Tre's name?

"Is there a reason you came back?" Tre rudely interrupted. He wasn't feeling particularly warm toward her.

"It's time you came home," Skylin told him as though it was a done deal and he was expected to jump up and leave.

Rin let out a gasp. She had been afraid of this very thing for the past two years. "Why didn't you tell us this the last time you came?" Rin asked, her voice quivering. She held back tears that were ready to fall.

Skylin looked at Rin like crying was something foreign to her. "Last time I just learned I had a twin brother and had to see for myself. I just didn't believe it was true." She continued to watch Rin. She looked as if she might run when the first tear fell.

"I can't leave my mother alone. It's not safe, and I have responsibilities in the village." Tre was not going to be told what to do by this girl, even if she was his sister.

"Cerra and Koda have kept watch over the years to keep you both safe. Rin can't stay here when you leave because they won't be here to protect her," Skylin agreed. Tre was shocked.

Skylin turned to Tre. "You have to come home. Bad things are going to happen, and only you can stop them." Then the reason for her attitude came out as she grumbled, "It's not fair. I'm the oldest, but I can't rule, because I'm a girl. That was the reason you were kept hidden and then sent away. You would have been killed. Only a 'king' can rule in Fairland."

Tre stuttered, "Rule—like—like a king? Is that what you're saying?" Everything was moving too fast, and he was especially anxious about this ruling part.

"I'll explain on the way. We need to go. We can't be seen during the day hour." Skylin stood up and turned toward the door, ready to leave.

"Stop. I'm not going anywhere and leaving my mother." Tre stood up so fast that his chair crashed backward. His face turned red. He was angry at how she expected him to leave his mother and his home at her order.

Rin stepped beside Tre and put her hand on his arm. "I can move into the bakery. Ely and Joan are getting old and need someone there at night." She took Tre's face in her hands and said, "I've know from the beginning that this day would come and I would have to give you up. You have a destiny to fulfill and a family that needs your help."

"You are my family, and you would never abandon me in a river!" Tre was trying to stay calm but without success. He was upset with the way things were going; he felt he had no say in the matter.

"I'll move to the bakery in the morning and let everyone know that you have gone on a trip," Rin reasoned with him.

"What about Little Flock? The village needs protection." Tre's mind was in a whirl finding excuses not to leave his home and everything familiar to him.

"Dellis is able to lead Little Flock and protect the village," Rin countered.

Skylin picked up the old red blanket that Rin had placed on Tre's bed. "I had one just like this," she exclaimed and then tore off one end of the blanket and handed it to Rin. "If you're in trouble and need Tre, hang this cloth in the tree where Koda kept watch. Now we must hurry to get back before light." Skylin picked up her staff, took the matching one from the corner of the hut, and tossed it to her twin. "Don't forget to bring that knife you dropped. You may need it." She grinned at Tre and stepped out of the hut.

Skylin was a bundle of laughs, Tre grumbled to himself as he followed her outside. He turned and looked at Rin, who had tears running down her cheeks, and at the old hut that had been the only home he had ever known. Somehow everything had changed without his agreement, and now he was heading into an unknown future.

The Twins of Fairland

Part 2

The Hidden

Chapter 6

Tre hurried to keep up with his twin and her large cat. The monstrous beast quickly led the way through the forest and down the back of the mountain. When Skylin finally stopped, waiting for the cat to scout ahead, Tre was breathing hard. *The girl*, that was how he thought of her, not as his sister, was not winded at all. The girl was in great physical shape, which made him wonder about her as he gulped for air. All the girls from the village helped their mothers around the house with things like sweeping and cooking, not tramping through forests with large cats and carrying heavy staffs. Tre looked at the staff he carried and felt its weight. It was carved from a hard wood unfamiliar to him. It would make a great weapon because of its size and strength. Another thing that puzzled him was how the girl spoke to the cat; it seemed to understand her. There were times she would signal with her staff to wait while the cat went on ahead, as though she knew its thoughts too. Tre had to admit there were a lot of strange things about the girl.

"Be careful; the tree is slippery from all the moss," Skylin said as they stepped out of the woods. These were the first real words she had said since he and she left the hut, except when she ordered him to stop, wait, or hurry up. Tre could see a deep gorge that separated the mountain they had crossed from a large valley below. The far end of the valley was where the tall purple mountains began. A tree had fallen or been pushed over across the gorge to form a bridge. The twins stood on a high, rocky ledge, and Tre could hear the sound of a river rushing below in a series of dangerous rapids. There was enough light from the moon to see to cross. "If you fall, you're on your own," Skylin smugly said and then stepped onto the slippery bridge. Using her staff for balance, she easily made her way to the other side. She jumped to the ground and turned to watch him come across.

Tre thought the girl would be delighted if he slipped and fell into the rushing river below. He balanced the staff in his hands. He had closely watched the girl use her staff for balance as she crossed the slippery bridge. Tre took a deep breath to steady his nerves. On the first step, his foot slipped. The smooth moccasins he wore to run the mountain trails were not ideal for slippery trees. He used the staff to steady his balance and carefully took a second step. He concentrated on each step until he made it across. "Don't look so disappointed," he told the girl when he stepped off the bridge to the other side. Skylin lifted her eyebrows and shrugged her shoulders like it didn't matter to her one bit if he fell to his death or not. Then, without a word, she turned and continued trailing the large cat into the valley below.

Tre had never been this far from home. He was amazed when they entered a large meadow. It had remained hidden from the villagers because of the rugged mountains and the river. Tre again wondered if the tree had been purposely pushed across the narrow gorge to allow Skylin to find him. He paused for a moment, thinking about how the meadow would be a great place to grow crops and raise animals. The winters would be mild in the meadow, without the extreme cold and snow in the mountains. Tre knew the villagers stayed hidden away high in the mountain because of their fear of the lowlander raiders. He sighed at the lost opportunity to bring his mother and the villagers to this meadow to live.

As they crossed the meadow the grass reached Tre's waist. He stepped beside Skylin, pointed with his staff, and asked, "The purple mountains—is that where we're going?"

"Yes," she tersely answered.

"How do we get over them? I was told there is no way to get through." Tre was curious to find out.

"Wait and you'll see," Skylin abruptly replied. She wasn't making it easy to have a conversation.

"I thought you were going to explain everything on the way," Tre reminded her. He was heading into the unknown and didn't like the feeling. He was persistent and continued asking her questions. "Is there a village with people? What about our parents?" He had different parents, and the thought was strange. Rin was the only family he had ever known, until now.

"Old Nanny and Mallrok are waiting for us. They will explain everything," Skylin answered and continued tromping through the tall grass.

"You said 'bad things' would happen. What bad things?" Tre asked as he walked through the grass behind her. Skylin suddenly stopped, and Tre bumped into her.

She turned around and grumbled, "Do you always ask so many questions?"

He leaned in, coming face to face with her, and yelled, "You would too if you were me. I just learned that I'm not who I thought I was and I have a family I never knew I had and if I don't come with you, bad things are going to happen. I think you would be asking questions too!"

Skylin brushed aside her brother's outburst and admitted, "There is a secret entrance through the mountains." She turned away and continued walking after the large cat. Tre gave up; trying to get any further information from her was useless.

Finally they stopped where a waterfall crashed to the ground, creating a crystal blue lake. On one end the lake overflowed and formed a small stream. Tre studied the stream as it ran downhill. Fourteen years ago, his small craft was put into the stream, and he was sent on his first journey to the unknown. Now he had returned to the same place on his second journey to the unknown.

The flapping of wings above Tre's head startled him, and he instinctively ducked. The big owl, which Skylin called Koda, landed on a large boulder beside the waterfall and folded his wings. Up close the great bird was impressive. His feathers were a dark brown with a sprinkling of orange, and he had piercing black eyes that missed nothing. His curved beak looked as sharp as Tre's knife, and Tre was sure the big owl could inflict major damage with it. The owl's feet had huge talons that could carry away a large deer. Koda blinked his eyes and nodded his head. Was it a signal? Could his sister understand the bird too? Tre was shocked; he had thought of *the girl* as *my sister.*

"This way." Skylin motioned as she stepped into the water, using her staff to prod the bottom of the lake to avoid deep holes. She disappeared behind the large boulder where Koda perched. Tre stepped into the water, which rushed quickly past his knees. Like his sister, Tre used the staff to maneuver his way around the lake and squeezed behind the large boulder. The owl never moved as it watched him. Tre was hesitant around the large brown bird, although it had been a constant part of his childhood. He glanced at Koda, wondering if he should say something, because he sure couldn't read its thoughts like Skylin seemed able to do. Communicating with large scary animals was one skill this twin didn't inherit.

It was dark behind the waterfall, but Tre could make out a rock ledge. The ledge was slippery when he stepped on it. He inched toward the back and almost missed seeing a narrow opening on one side. Of course his sister did not wait to guide him. Tre cautiously started down the narrow opening, keeping one hand placed against the mountain side to guide him. When he stepped out of the tunnel, Skylin was waiting for him with arms folded. "Stay close and be quiet," she ordered. Tre was quite fed up with her bossy behavior. He couldn't remember anyone he knew who was as rude as she.

Skylin led the way down a narrow path to where the large cat waited in the trees, and together they moved forward. It was quiet, only the soft tread of their steps broke the stillness. They travelled a short way when Tre saw the outline of a large building. It was dark, but he could tell it was bigger than any of the houses in his village. He did not see any other buildings close by. The cat stopped on the path that hugged the tree line. Skylin stopped beside the cat, patted his head, and whispered something. Tre could tell she was fond of Cerra and the big cat protective of her. He heard a faint "who," and perched on a tree limb above them was the large owl. Koda must have flown over the high mountain to meet them here.

A door opened in the dark building and light flickered out. Skylin hurried toward the door. Tre hesitated. Then he took a large breath, squared his shoulders, and followed after Skylin. An old woman stood in the doorway waiting for them. She gave Skylin a warm hug and said, "We've been worried you wouldn't make it back before light." She spoke with a strange lilt in her voice, making it hard for Tre to understand her. The old woman took Tre's arm and pulled him inside. She shut and latched the door. "Let me look at you," she exclaimed and led him further into the room. From the light inside, she took in his appearance. "You are a sight for the eyes. It's been far too long, young prince." She pulled him into her arms and hugged him tight. Tre hoped she didn't smother him and wasn't sure what to do or say. *Who is this old woman?* he wondered, and the "young prince" comment worried him. The old woman turned toward the fireplace, and Tre noticed there was someone seated there. "I thought this day would never come," she said to the stranger, taking a rag from her pocket and wiping her teary eyes.

A man dressed in a long white robe stood up. He was tall and had a gray beard. Tre wasn't sure what to think, as he had never seen anyone dressed like this. The man walked over and examined Tre closely. "You have grown healthy and strong. The resemblance to your twin is remarkable. Come and sit. I'm sure you are tired from your long journey." He motioned to the chair by the fireplace. Tre was exhausted both physically and emotionally and collapsed in the chair. "Let me introduce myself. I am Mallrok." His manner was formal, and he bowed from the waist. He gestured toward the old woman. "This is Veerna. She is your and Skylin's nanny and was your mother's nanny as well."

The old woman shuffled forward, grinning widely, making the lines in her face even deeper. "It was so hard to let you go, but we could not hide you any longer. Kross was becoming suspicious. The animals kept watch and reported to Mallrok of your safety. We are so thankful you have returned." She ran the sentences together, adding to Tre's confusion.

Skylin took the old nanny by the arm and led her to a wooden bench across from the chair where Tre sat. She helped the old nanny sit down. Tre could see his twin loved the old woman, which was a big change from the surly girl he had observed. Maybe she did have a nicer side. Mallrok announced, "It will be dawn soon, and I have to leave and make plans. Prince Naveen, I want you to understand how critical your return is to the kingdom."

Tre stared at Mallrok. He was confused and explained, "My name is Tre."

"I understand that is the name the woman who found you gave you," Mallrok responded.

"You mean my mother." Tre was adamant and was not going to let Rin's part in his life be brushed aside.

"Your name is not as important as the role you must assume at the next Celebration of Harvest. It's the yearly feast after the harvest is in, and all marriages for the year are performed. Kross has chosen his second wife and is boasting of a son, which will seal his rule of the kingdom," Mallrok explained as he moved around the room.

Tre tried to understand everything but was confused by all the names and events. Mallrok turned, noticed the anxious look on Tre's face, and continued. "Kross has left Skylin alone because a girl cannot assume the throne, even though he would as soon kill her." He paused and then added, "You both resemble your mother very much." The smile he gave the twins was wistful.

Tre was still confused and asked, "Who is Kross?"

"It's a sad story. Kross is your father's younger brother and was madly in love with your mother, Queen Laurel.

When your mother chose to marry your father, King Naveen, Kross's hatred turned him evil. He plotted revenge and killed your father before your birth. After Skylin was born no one knew there was another child, but hours later you were born. Veerna delivered you and sent for me. A daughter could survive Kross's wrath, but never a son. You would inherit the throne and rule when you turned fifteen."

"We kept you hidden for almost a year, but Kross's guards were becoming suspicious and began watching Veerna. We had to get you out of the kingdom. Veerna built a small watercraft, and I released it in the stream and sent Koda and Cerra to watch over you. We keep Skylin away from the castle and town as much as possible. Everyone thinks she is a wild and unruly child." He paused and looked at Skylin, adding, "Which she is most of the time. She can beat all the young men at the summer games, from riding horses to throwing lances." That explained a lot about his twin; she had been raised alone and outside normal home conditions to keep her safe. She ran wild in the woods with her cat. Anyone who would dare to harm her would have to get past Cerra, and Tre knew that even an army would lose a battle with the monstrous cat.

Mallrok went to the window and looked out. "It's getting light, and I must go. I don't want to be seen here." He turned to Tre. "You must stay inside, and don't let anyone see you." He pointed to Skylin and said, "You stay here too, and stay out of trouble. When I return there is someone I want both of you to meet." He kissed Veerna's cheek and said, "Soon, dear nanny, many wrongs will be made right. Wish me luck." Then he left.

*　　*　　*

Tre peeked out the window to get a look at his surroundings. The sun was high and the sky a bright blue. After Mallrok left, Tre followed Skylin up a long set of stairs to the top floor of the building, where two cots were placed. They each collapsed in one and were asleep within minutes.

Now rested, Tre was curious about this hidden kingdom. From the window, he could see a large valley with rows and rows of crops in shades of green, yellow, and orange. There were workers in the fields, and Tre watched, amazed at the amount of the harvest. The few crops they were able to grow on the high mountain were surrounded by fences to keep wild animals from eating their meager bounty.

The smell of cooking drifted up, and his stomach reminded him he had not eaten in over a day. Remembering the warning from Mallrok to stay hidden, Tre listened, and, hearing no voices, he cautiously crept down the stairs. He saw Old Nanny standing at the fireplace stirring something in a large black pot. Looking down from the landing, Tre said, "That smells good."

The old nanny turned and smiled. "I wondered when you would be waking. Come down, come down, we are alone." She motioned for him to sit at the table. "Your sister has gone out but should be back soon. She was tired of waiting for you to wake. I told her you had a long day and a lot to take in and needed your rest. Eat. I'm sure you're famished." She placed a large bowl of stew in front of him filled with all kinds of vegetables he had never seen before. Tre picked up a spoon and eagerly began to eat.

Chapter 7

Two days had passed since Tre's return home. His old nanny had told him more about his family. Tre had inherited his name from his father, King Naveen, being the oldest son. When Laurel's father died, she became queen but could not rule Fairland. According to their custom, the ruler must be a king, and she had to choose between the brothers Naveen and Kross. She picked Naveen for her husband and king. Veerna told Tre that anyone who knew the two brothers said Laurel made the right choice.

Hurt and angry, Kross turned against Naveen and Laurel. He left the valley and hid away in the forest. King Naveen searched for Kross for days but could not find him. When Laurel became with child the whole kingdom was excited. The Celebration of Harvest had begun, and with the added anticipation of the arrival of a royal baby, it was a very special time in Fairland. One afternoon during the festival, King Naveen left the castle. No one knew where he went, and he never returned. After weeks of searching, it was finally declared the king must be dead. The queen was crushed by Naveen's disappearance, and her health became fragile. Only the thought of the child she carried kept her alive during those dark days.

After King Naveen was officially proclaimed dead, Kross returned to the valley with an army of heavily armed men and swiftly took control of the castle. Fairland was a peaceful kingdom and not prepared to defend itself from attack. The few castle guards were either killed or locked away in cells. The queen was very ill, and Mallrok and Veerna moved her from the castle to this house, where Veerna lived. Veerna took care of the queen until she gave birth. When Skylin was born, the queen was so weak that everyone assumed she had died. Hours later Tre was born. When Old Nanny saw the baby was a boy, she hid him and sent for Mallrok. With Kross in rule of the kingdom, they knew he would have the boy killed. Mallrok decided to tell everyone the queen had died in childbirth. Old Nanny kept the baby boy hidden until it became critical to send him away to keep him alive. From here, Tre knew the story. Skylin was raised by Old Nanny, and Rin had rescued Tre from the river and raised him as her own son. As Tre listened to Old Nanny, he meant to ask where his mother was buried, but forgot.

Against Old Nanny's stern warning, Skylin dressed Tre as a crop worker to give him a tour of the town and the long fertile valley that he could see from the window upstairs. She assured old nanny they would not go near the castle and would come back if she saw Kross or any of his guards. As they walked toward town, Skylin told Tre she had heard old stories that, many years past, Fairland held yearly trades with the mountain villagers and the lowlanders. At the end of the growing season, they would come together to trade crops, animals, and crafts. But something had happened, and they began to fight. Skylin wasn't sure of the details, but the different tribes were called lowlanders, farlanders, and mountain dwellers. The people in the hidden kingdom were the farlanders, and over the years the name changed to Fairland. Of course, it wasn't very fair any more with Kross acting as king.

Tre knew the stories of the lowlanders. They were cruel and mean and raided and killed the mountain people. They enslaved their captors, sentencing them to a life of hard labor and brutal treatment. Tre could not imagine anyone wanting to be friends or trade with such monsters. He had never heard there were people living behind the purple mountains and asked Skylin how long the Fairlanders had been hidden away in the valley. Skylin said she wasn't sure, but longer than five first-borns. Tre figured it was over one hundred years since the entrance to Fairland had been sealed.

Tre was amazed at the size and richness of the valley kingdom. The number of crops being harvested was vast; the cattle and horses that grazed in lush green grass were fat and healthy, so different from the few scrawny animals in his village. The horses amazed him the most. He had only seen one horse in the mountain village, and it was so old no one dared to ride it. They left it alone to eat and sleep. Skylin said riding horses was her favorite pastime. All the homes they passed on the way to the town had goats in the yards for milk and cheese.

As he watched the people work, Tre noticed that no one smiled or sang or shouted greetings to each other. Rin always sang as she worked, whether around their small hut or at the bakery preparing the day's bread. She made a chore into a game with a song. Moon, Tre smiled as he remembered the young girl with the long brown hair— Rin taught Moon many of the songs she had learned from her mother. Tre said Moon sang like a bird and would tease her, calling her Moon Bird. Then there was Axe. He was big and strong and didn't look any different from the other men, but he was mute and could only make grunting noises. Rin had taught him to whistle. Axe would mimic her singing, halting at first until he learned the tune. Then he would whistle each note perfectly. Everyone called him Axe because when they asked him his name, he crossed his arms on his chest in an X. Axe used hand signals to communicate, and most of the time he was able to make himself understood.

As the twins walked around the town, Tre figured it was at least four or five times as big as the mountain village. It was built around a large open square where Skylin said meetings and celebrations were held, but there had not been anything to celebrate for a long time. There were a variety of craftsmen, each with their own shop, but the large bakery amazed him the most. Tre peeked in the window and wanted to go inside to see if the loaves were like the ones Rin made, but Skylin would not let him. Tre had to stay in the shadows and keep his hood pulled over his head; she did not want anyone to get a good look at him and notice their resemblance. *Not that it would matter,* Tre thought. No one paid any attention to them and seemed to avoid Skylin, although he was sure everyone knew who she was. She stood out, different from the other girls in Fairland in her bearing, her dress, and her manner. The town was almost empty of people; the summer harvest had begun and everyone was required to help to bring in the crops.

Skylin told Tre the winters in the valley were mild because they were sheltered by the tall mountains. This was different from the harsh winters he shared with Rin, when having enough wood on hand to keep from freezing on the long, cold nights was a daily task. Skylin said she loved snow and tracking through it with Cerra. Cerra did not come into town, but stayed near the edge, always watching Skylin. The twins left the town, hiked up the mountain, and sat looking out at the large valley. Tre saw

41

Koda perched nearby in a tree and asked his sister how she could understand the animals. She thought a minute and said she could feel what they wanted from a sound or movement, and when she could not see Cerra, she always knew when he was near. Tre had tried to communicate with Koda, closing his eyes and listening hard, but he always came up with nothing. His mind stayed blank. He could communicate with the log they sat on just as easily.

During the past two days, the relationship between the twins had improved. Skylin wasn't as curt in her manner toward Tre, and he was able to go longer between the times when he wanted to strangle her. He was beginning to like her, which he initially thought would never happen. Skylin taught him some moves with the staff to defend himself, and he showed her how to throw his knife. She caught on quickly and said she would get a knife of her own. *Why would she need a knife in this safe valley?* he wondered. Tre pointed to the markings on the staff and asked her about them. She said the largest one that looked like a triangle with a circle around the top stood for Fairland, the kingdom in the mountain. The three squiggle lines represented the mountain stream, and the symbol that looked like two connected circles represented the eternal rule of the king. She traced the symbol with her finger showing him there was no end; it went on forever.

Koda, in a nearby tree, gave a "who," and Skylin turned to Tre and said they must get back. It was strange how comfortable Tre had become having Cerra and Koda around. As they walked back to Old Nanny's house, Skylin asked Tre about his childhood. He told her about the mountain village and living in the small hut with Rin. It was a hard life when he thought about it, but they had been warm and happy, and he never went hungry. Rin had taken care of him as if he was her own child, even risking her own life when she found him. Tre told her about the children in the village and the funny things they did, and Skylin laughed out loud. It was the first time he had heard her really laugh with mirth, rather than at his expense. He told her everything he could think of about his village: about the threat of the lowlanders raiding the village and having to be on constant watch during the warm months; how the boys of Little Flock practiced until they were as skilled as the men; about Axe not being able to speak but perfectly whistling any tune he heard.

"I envy you," Skylin said sincerely. "Old Nanny and Mallrok didn't have time for games or fun." How very different their childhoods were: She had the wealth of a kingdom and all she wanted; he had the wealth of laughter and happiness. She stayed hidden away, afraid of being killed, and he was happy and carefree in the small hut.

As they came to the home of Old Nanny, Tre noticed how quiet it was and saw men hiding in the trees. Old Nanny was waiting by the door and hurried them inside; she shut and locked the door and pulled a curtain across the window. Something strange was going on, but Tre wasn't sure what. Skylin went to Old Nanny, put her arm around her bent shoulders, and looked at Tre as if to say, *Do you know what is happening?*

Mallrok was there and motioned for them to sit. Then he began talking about their birth, their father disappearing, Kross and his men taking over the kingdom, the iron-fisted rule for the last fourteen years, the people being deprived of their earnings and weapons, how the guards locked down the town at night. He paused to gather his thoughts and said, "Next week, after the crops are in, the yearly Celebration of Harvest begins. Kross is going to announce his marriage during the celebration. No one is sure what happened to his first wife and was afraid to ask when she went missing. She was not able to have children, and without a son, he can't officially rule over Fairland." Mallrok walked to the window and looked out. Then he said, "Next week we plan to proclaim Tre as the rightful king."

Tre was stunned and gasped. "I can't. I can't be a king. I don't even know my way around this place." He thought he was going to pass out.

Mallrok placed a hand on his shoulder and said, "You won't be alone and your people need you."

Skylin stood up and declared, "You have my full support. It's time Kross is defeated and we stop living in fear." Her voice was firm.

"But I'm no king," Tre stammered.

"But you're a born leader," Skylin answered back, looking her brother in the eyes. Tre felt a shiver run along his spine at the steel determination he saw in his sister's expression.

Mallrok walked to the stairway and motioned for someone to come down. "There is someone else that will help you." He reached out his hand, and it was taken by a person waiting on the stairs. Then he announced, "Children, meet your mother."

Chapter 8

Tre and Skylin rushed to the stairs. They were stunned, and shock covered their faces. Neither of them could believe what Mallrok had said. Their mother was alive, when all along they thought she was dead. The woman on the stairs who grasped Mallrok's hand seemed almost ethereal like an angel in a flowing white dress. She was slim and as tall as Mallrok, with long blond hair braided around her head that fell loosely down her back. Her piercing blue eyes studied the twins. She smiled as she stepped forward, and, with arms held out, she said, "My children, at last we are together." Her voice was warm and soft.

Skylin was visibly shaken and uttered, "Mother," as she slowly stepped forward. Tre just stood and stared at the beautiful woman, trying to come to understand that his real mother had been alive all this time. He could only think of her as a queen, both her manner and look so regal. Again Tre was faced with a staggering situation. With Skylin folded in her arms, the woman looked at Tre. Softly she said, "I know you have had many changes to deal with in the past few days, and I understand you're hesitant in accepting me as your mother."

Tre quickly stepped forward and stammered, "It's not that, but you're alive and a real queen. I don't know what to do or say!" trying to explain his odd behavior.

Queen Laurel took Tre in her outstretched arm and drew him close. "Just be yourself," she assured him. Then she hugged both twins tightly and said, "I could not be more proud of the both of you. I am so happy that I lived to see this day and hold my children in my arms." Tears ran down the queen's face.

Mallrok led the three of them to the large wooden table and pulled out chairs for them to sit. Old Nanny's eyes sparkled with joy. The secret that she kept for fourteen years had been revealed. Once they were all seated Queen Laurel said, "We have so much to catch up on. Although I must admit that I have been kept informed about both of you by Mallrok. Skylin and Tre, you have grown into amazing children. Or should I say adults? It seems that is what you are." The queen reached out and squeezed both of the twins' hands.

As Old Nanny fixed food for their dinner, Mallrok explained, "After Tre was born—" He paused, looked at Tre, and said, "The queen has instructed everyone to call you by that name." Then he continued with his story. With the queen so near death and Old Nanny with the twins to care for, they decided to move the queen to a hidden cabin high in the mountain. He repeated the story Old Nanny had already told Trey, of the wooden watercraft and releasing it in the mountain stream and how Koda and Cerra were sent to keep watch so no harm would come to the child. He noted how fate stepped in when Rin found the boy and carried him to the mountain village. It was over two years before the queen was strong enough to care for herself, and by then Kross had taken control of the kingdom. Mallrok looked at the queen and Old Nanny and said, "We all decided that it would be best to keep the queen's survival a secret. Tre was being cared for by Rin, and Skylin was here with Veerna."

Puzzled, Skylin asked, "How did you get away without having a funeral for mother?" She had seen the place in the valley where the Fairlanders honored and buried their loved ones who had passed on.

Old Nanny sat a basket of bread on the table. She looked a Skylin and answered, "Mallrok told everyone that it was too sad, with the loss of King Naveen and now the death of Queen Laurel, to hold a royal funeral. Instead he called for a week of mourning. A couple of men from town dug a grave on the hillside." Old Nanny pointed out the window toward the mountain.

She sure had her secrets, because Skylin had never known of the hillside grave. "But what did you bury?" Skylin was confused.

Old Nanny chuckled loudly and replied, "My old goat had just died, so I wrapped him up in a blanket and buried him. A goat for a queen!" She cackled at her joke, her grin toothless.

The idea of burying a goat in a grave intended for the queen was so bizarre that everyone started laughing. All the tension at the table dissolved, and the rest of the evening was spent learning about Tre's childhood, Queen Laurel's determination to get well, and Skylin roaming the mountains with Cerra. After the queen and twins were finished telling their stories, Mallrok shocked the twins again. He told them he had been working with some men to form an army to overthrow Kross. "They have been secretly meeting in the mountains and making weapons. Kross and his gang of guards have become lazy, thinking no one in Fairland would dare to go against him. In two days the Celebration of Harvest will begin, and the army is ready."

Mallrok stood and took the queen's hand. He bowed and said, "The rightful queen will once more reign in Fairland. Now I must go. There will be men standing guard in the trees. Stay inside until the festival, and do not let anyone see you," he firmly cautioned them.

"This year we will have something to celebrate." Old nanny's voice cracked with resolve. She raised her arm, and hit one of the pots hanging above the fireplace with a large spoon. The loud clang echoed around the room like a battle cry.

* * *

During the two days before the festival Old Nanny kept a watchful eye out the window. As they waited, Tre questioned Queen Laurel. "You said Skylin and I have gifts. Skylin has the skills of a warrior and can understand animals. What do I have?"

His mother laughed. "You are too modest, Tre. Your father was the same way. He was a born leader, and everyone loved him and would follow him to the Earth's end. You have his same qualities. Look at how you took a handful of boys and turned them into an army. What did you call them?"

Tre smiled, thinking of the effort it took to turn the village boys into an army. "My mother—err, I mean Rin— she named them 'Little Flock.' She said they followed me around like a flock of birds." Tre missed Rin and his friends in the village and wondered if she had moved to the bakery and if Little Flock was keeping up their daily drills.

As the time for the festival came near, Tre's apprehension increased. Once again he was heading into an unknown situation. He watched Skylin pace about Old

Nanny's house, pausing often to look out the window. She didn't seem worried but anxious for the battle ahead.

*   *   *

Tre pulled the hood over his head. Old Nanny draped the queen in one of her old cloaks and tied a scarf around her head to hide her features. If anyone was suspicious, it would be hard to identify them in the crowd of people. Mallrok's instructions were to wait until the town square was full of people before leaving Old Nanny's house. He assured the queen she would be safe and had assigned men to protect her. They were to make their way to the side of the wooden platform Kross had built so everyone could see him when he made his marriage announcement.

Skylin was going as herself; she had no need to hide. She tightened the belt around her waist so her new weapon was secure. She now had a knife with a carved wooden handle that matched her staff and could hit any target she aimed at. Tre was glad she was his sister and not his enemy. He would not want to do battle with her. He knew he wouldn't be the winner. Skylin and Tre were as tall as most of the men in Fairland and both were strong and fit. They were the mirror image of each other and yet opposite in other ways. Together they were the Twins of Fairland.

Skylin handed Tre his staff and said, "Keep this with you. You will need it before this day is over." Tre took the staff, and there was no doubt in his mind he would use it against Kross or his guards if they threatened Queen Laurel. Tre had become very fond of the sweet-mannered woman who was his real mother. He was becoming comfortable with the thought that he was part of a family and had a new mother and a twin sister. Old Nanny filled the grandmother role, and Mallrok seemed like an uncle always watchful for their safety.

The town square was packed with people moving around and quietly talking. Their hushed whispers rose into muffled noise. As quietly as possible, Queen Laurel, Tre, and Old Nanny made their way to the side of the wooden platform. Tre walked on one side of his mother and Old Nanny on the other. They kept their heads bowed to cover their faces. Skylin walked alone, not wanting to draw attention to them. Most everyone acknowledged Skylin with a nod, although no one spoke to her. They just bowed their heads and moved out of her way. She was strikingly dressed with the staff and knife like a warrior princess. Tre glanced over at his twin and realized Skylin was as regal in her way as Queen Laurel was in hers.

A hush rippled through the crowded square as Kross stepped forward. Tre's first look at his uncle sent a chill down his spine. He was dressed all in black, and a large sword hung from his waist. Dark was Tre's first impression—dark features, dark hair, dark soul. The scowl on his face was menacing, and his eyes seemed to radiate evil. Tre understood why everyone was frightened in Kross's presence. Tre counted twenty heavily armed guards surrounding him. Kross purposefully climbed to the top of the platform, stopping on each step and glaring out at the crowd of people as though he could tell if anyone was missing and ensure they would pay the price of not showing up to give him honor.

Tre looked around for Mallrok but did not see him. He kept a firm grip on his mother's arm, worried that she might faint. Queen Laurel turned and looked at him. Her expression was not one of fear, but of fury—not one of a weakling, but of a warrior queen. Tre knew that expression well; he had seen it many times on the face of his twin sister. His mother was no coward, nor was Skylin. *And neither am I*, he determined. Tre firmly gripped his staff, ready for battle.

Kross raised his arms signaling for silence, even though everyone had stopped their hushed whispers at his arrival. "The Celebration of Harvest has begun. The crops are in, and the yield is greater this year than last," he announced in a loud voice. The tired and haggard looks on the villager's faces suggested they knew the hard work involved in bringing the crops to harvest and the beatings that would be theirs if the crops failed. Yes, it was a greater yield this year, but not for them. They would only get what Kross decided to give them. A handful of people cheered; they were his guards. Kross strutted across the platform with one hand resting on the large gleaming sword. He turned and looked across the crowd and then continued. "This year I will be taking a new wife, and with the birth of my son, I will be proclaiming myself king of Fairland." There was not a sound from the crowd.

The hush continued until a voice in the back of the crowd cried out, "How can you be king of Fairland when there is currently a queen and a prince of age to assume the throne?" The stunned crowd parted as Mallrok, dressed in his finest robe and carrying a staff that matched the twins', stepped forward.

"What did he say?"; "What queen?"; "There is no prince"— these questions came from the crowd. The clamor became louder as Mallrok stepped upon the platform and faced Kross.

Kross was enraged, his face red as he sneered and said, "What trick is this, Mallrok?"

Mallrok turned and faced the bewildered crowd. Loudly he proclaimed, "The rightful rulers of Fairland are

Queen Laurel and her children, Prince Naveen and Princess Skylin." The stunned crowd watched as Queen Laurel removed the scarf and cloak and climbed the steps to the platform. Gasps of recognition came from the villagers at seeing their beloved queen alive and standing before them.

Kross stumbled backward at the sight of Queen Laurel. His black eyes bulged with hate, realizing the queen really was alive. When Tre and Skylin stepped up beside their mother, Kross screamed at his guards. "Kill them! Kill them all!" he loudly shrieked.

As Kross's guards drew their weapons and started toward the queen, the army of men hidden in the crowd dropped their coats and readied their weapons. A barrage of arrows flew straight at the guards on the platform. Frightened men and women ran from the town square as the secret army ran forward to challenge Kross and his guards. As the arrows hit the platform, Kross's guards turned to escape, but it didn't matter which direction the guards ran; the platform was now surrounded by the secret army. Kross continued screaming at the guards, turning in circles on the platform. His face had turned dark red, and spit clung to his black beard, making him look like a rabid animal. The army tightened the circle around the platform, not allowing the guards to escape, determined to end the rule of the evil Kross.

It was chaos: people were running in every direction and screaming; Kross was shrieking at his guards; the guards ran from one side of the platform to the other trying to escape the deadly arrows. Mallrok hurried Queen Laurel off the platform to the safety of her guards. Tre was helping his mother down the steps, afraid she would fall and be trampled, when suddenly he was jerked backward. Tre stumbled and fell. He turned to get up and saw Kross standing over him. Kross had drawn his large sword and was lifting it high. In that moment Tre knew his father had been killed by Kross's sword. He could feel his father's presence with him. Tre tried to turn away from certain death when Kross stepped on his shoulder, pinning him down.

The look on Kross's face was one of pure hatred. As he swung his sword in a downward motion toward Tre, Kross suddenly jerked backward, and the sword dropped from his hands. The expression on Kross's face changed from evil to intense shock and pain. His hands clutched at his chest. A carved wood—handled knife was embedded in his heart. Blood began to ooze from the wound and drip between Kross's fingers, staining his shirt red. It was only seconds but it seemed an eternity to Tre. Time had stopped. Even the deafening noise all around him did not penetrate Tre's hearing.

Skylin leaped onto the platform and with a mighty swing of her staff hit Kross, sending him flying off the platform. Kross landed in the dirt, slumped over. He was dead. Skylin reached out a hand to Tre and yelled, "The battle isn't over brother!" Tre grabbed her hand, jumped up, and ran to the back of the platform where Kross's guards were making a final stand against the secret army. "Are you going to use that knife?" Skylin shouted at Tre.

"Yes," Tre shouted back. He grabbed his old knife and threw it, directly hitting the captain of the guards. With their captain dead, the guards lost their advantage, and the secret army quickly defeated them. When all the guards were dead, shouts of victory from the secret army announced Fairland's freedom from Kross's evil rule.

Skylin ran to the front of the platform and down the steps. She rushed to the slumped body of Kross, and, using her boot, she pushed him over, reached down, and pulled out her knife. "I wanted to make sure I got this back," she exclaimed and looked at the still form of Kross, satisfied that her years of living in fear were over.

"You saved my life. He was ready to kill me!" Tre gasped as he realized how close he came to dying. This was his first real fight. The hours of training with Little Flock and practicing on stuffed dummies and targets somehow didn't prepare him for a real life-or-death situation. He shook his head to clear these thoughts. "Where's mother?" he asked his sister. He had lost sight of her when Kross grabbed him. The twins began pushing their way through the crowd of people, who were beginning to realize the rule of Kross was over. It was like they were frozen and didn't know what to do now that Kross was dead.

"People of Fairland," Mallrok shouted from the middle of the town square, "the reign of Kross is over, and Queen Laurel has taken back the throne. Prepare for a feast tonight in the castle to celebrate the harvest and our beloved queen's return home." It was what the people needed to hear, and they started cheering and raising their fists in victory. Suddenly Skylin and Tre were heroes. Everyone wanted to thank them, hold their hands, or pat them on the back. Smiles brightened everyone's face, so different from the people Tre had seen before. Mallrok hurried the twins to a large path that led to the castle. The entrance had been blocked since Kross had taken rule. Now the large gate was open. "Your mother waits inside," Mallrok said and pushed the twins forward.

The Celebration of Harvest feast was in progress; everyone was laughing and eating. There was more food than Tre had seen in his entire life. The palace glowed with hundreds of candles. It reminded Tre of twinkling stars in the night sky. The people were overjoyed at the sight of their queen shining as bright as a star herself. Somehow Queen Laurel had convinced Skylin to trade her warrior outfit for a shimmering blue gown, and Skylin glowed in her royal clothes. Tre looked at his finely made shirt with real buttons and tailored pants. He had never seen or worn anything like it before. He ran his hands over his legs, marveling at how smooth the fabric was. He had eaten until he could not hold another bite. Mallrok had everyone laughing at the stories he told. Old Nanny was busy giving orders to the cooks and loving every minute of her new position. Tre could not imagine a happier time or place. It was like no one had a care in the world. Everything was right. Everyone was happy.

A noise startled Tre, and he turned to look out the wide door that opened onto the outside balcony. It was Koda. He had flown into the castle and landed on the balcony railing, flapping his large wings for balance. It wasn't the large owl that caused Tre to jump up, knocking over his chair, but the bright red piece of cloth that hung from his beak. The same cloth Skylin had torn from his baby blanket and told Rin to hang on the tree if Rin ever needed him. Tre ran to Koda, grasp the cloth, and cried out, "Mother!"

Chapter 9

At Tre's loud cry of "Mother!" the large banquet hall went quiet and everyone turned to look at him, wondering what was happening. Skylin recognized the piece of red blanket, leaped from the table, and ran to her brother. She knew something terrible must have happened to cause Rin to send for Tre so soon. She counted the days since they had left the old hut. It had only been seven days, but it seemed longer because so much had happened in the short time.

Stunned, Tre looked at his sister and said, "I must go. Something is wrong." His face had lost all color, and Skylin sensed his worry. Queen Laurel and Mallrok rushed to where the twins stood.

"What is going on?" Queen Laurel asked. She couldn't understand what had terrified Tre now that the battle was won. Skylin quickly explained to their mother and Mallrok about the signal cloth that Koda had brought to Tre.

Tre moved toward the door. "I must go. My mother needs me."

Mallrok placed a hand on Tre's arm, stopping him. He cautioned, "It is night, and travelling will be dangerous. Wait for dawn. You'll be able to travel faster in the day."

Queen Laurel joined Mallrok's plea. "Please wait for first light. Besides, you need to prepare for the journey." She was concerned about him, and worry showed on her face.

Tre scowled. He was not happy about waiting until dawn. He needed to get to Rin fast. She would not have sent for him unless it was an emergency. "I'm coming too," Skylin said, placing her hand on her brother's arm. From the firm tone of her voice and look on her face, no one dared to argue with her decision. Finally, Tre agreed to wait until first light to start the long trip home.

Mallrok told him, "Cerra and Koda will accompany you. We don't know the dangers you may face or what caused Rin to send the signal." Tre and Skylin left the banquet hall together to prepare for the trip back to the mountain village.

Dawn was breaking over the tall purple-hued mountain, and the twins were ready to leave. They were dressed alike in brown pants and leather boots. Their shirts were dark green, and wide leather belts circled their waists. Both had knives secured in their belts and carried their staffs. Their long blond hair was tied in the back. One had to look close to tell them apart; even their movements matched.

Queen Laurel and Mallrok had travelled as far as Old Nanny's house to see the twins off on their journey. It had been a long night for Tre. He could not sleep from worrying about his mother and friends. Fear of what he might find, possibly the same fate as his mother's childhood village, kept him awake and restless. Skylin had packed supplies for their trip then filled the rest of the hours sharpening her knife. The sound of the blade hitting the polishing stone broke the silence while they waited for first light. Koda circled high overhead, and Cerra paced at the edge of the forest. Queen Laurel gave each twin a hug and held their hands. With a worried expression, she cautioned, "Be careful my children."

The early morning air held a chill and signaled the return of winter. Had the lowland raiders found the small village and made one final raid before the trails became too icy and dangerous for their horses? These thoughts raced through Tre's mind and increased his anxiety to reach the village. The twins ran at a steady pace once they were through the hidden passage in the mountain. Cerra led the way, and Koda kept watch, flying in large circles overhead. They reached the end of the long grassy meadow before the sun was at midpoint. Skylin suggested they rest before climbing the steep mountainside to the top where they would have to cross over the deep gorge on the slippery tree bridge.

"I'm sure Rin is okay. No one else knew about the signal." Skylin tried to comfort her brother.

"I've thought of that," Tre answered and then admitted his fear. "What about the others in the village, and Little Flock, and Moon?" Tre worried about the young girl that Rin had grown attached to. "Let's keep going." He decided and stood up and looked around for Cerra but didn't see him.

Skylin pointed with her staff and said, "This way." The uncanny way his twin could communicate with the large cat still baffled Tre.

Daylight was fading as the twins stopped in the tree line above the old hut that had been Tre's home for so long. The hut leaned to one side, ready to collapse at any moment, and its door hung open. The abandoned feeling that surrounded it saddened Tre. Skylin placed a hand on Cerra's back and told the large cat to stay and keep watch. Cerra gave a low growl, and Skylin answered, "If we run into trouble I'll call." She patted his large head. As the twins started down the hill, Tre could smell smoke. He hurried ahead, anxious to reach the village and find his mother.

Tre stopped at the edge of the village and stared at the burnt remnants that had once been homes and shops. The bakery and the small butcher shop were the only two buildings the fire had not reached. They were newer and built away from the other buildings, which were old and tightly crowded together for safety and warmth. *How had the fire started?* Tre wondered. He knew once the old wooden buildings caught fire, the villagers would have no way to put them out. It would consume their homes and belongings, and they could only stand and watch. A few of the animal pens were standing, but all the animals were missing, the chickens and cows all gone. The village depended on the milk and eggs to survive the winter months.

When Tre reached the bakery he saw people inside. He threw the door open and yelled, "Mother!" He went numb at what he saw. Villagers were slumped against the walls with bandages covering arms, legs, and heads. Blankets covered the floor where the more critically hurt lay moaning from their injuries. Tre looked around the room and counted at least twenty wounded men and women.

"Tre!" Rin shouted as she came down the stairs from the room where she now lived. Tre gasped at seeing a large red gash on the side of her face. Her arms were cut too. He knew these were defensive wounds; Rin had fought hard. She rushed to Tre and hugged him tight. Her voice was shaking. "They caught us by surprise. Snuck in from the back and started fires. While everyone tried to put out the fires, the rest of the raiders rode in from the trail. They must have been watching the village for weeks to plan an attack like this." She wiped at her tears and winced in pain. "They took Moon," she uttered and then wept in Tre's arms.

Skylin hurried forward, put her arm around Rin's shoulders, and led her to a wooden bench pushed up against the wall. Tre saw Dellis laying on one of the blankets, his left arm was bandaged and tied across his chest. Blood stained his shirt and pants. Tre made his way to him and knelt down. In a hushed voice he asked, "Dellis, what happened?" Dellis opened his eyes, and, seeing Tre, he sighed. "Little Flock fought hard, but too many warriors came in on horses." Tre put his arm around Dellis's shoulders and helped him sit up. "They snuck up behind the village and shot fire arrows into the buildings. With all the fires, everyone was confused, not realizing it was the raiders. I sounded the alarm, but it was too late." Dellis told Tre that Little Flock saved many of the villagers, and once the alarm sounded, they gathered their weapons and organized the way they had practiced. It saddened Tre to learn that three men and two women were killed in the raid. Many had been injured, but they would probably survive.

Dellis said the raiders had not expected resistance from the villagers or Little Flock's defense skills. Little Flock managed to kill two of the raiders and wound many others. Before the raiders retreated, they captured two women and Moon. Rin stood up. "We're going after them," she announced. "Soon as we get the injured treated, everyone that is able is going." Tre saw the old sword that Windel carried leaning against the wall and asked about the small boy. Sadly Rin said the leader of the raiders, a cruel warrior named Tulac, had put a spear through Windel's chest and laughed as he watched him die. Rin picked up Windel's sword and said, "I intend to kill Tulac." Tre wasn't shocked at Rin's words. He knew his mother harbored many horrid secrets about her captivity, and he did not doubt that she would seek revenge.

The following morning, everyone that was able gathered in the large open area where Little Flock practiced.

Rin and Dellis were planning to lead a group to rescue Moon and the two village women. The butcher who had given Tre his knife and taught him how to throw it was there. He said they could count on him going as well. His wife was one of the women taken prisoner, and he was determined to bring her home. There were three other men in the meeting. All were injured, but all volunteered to go. Axe and three of the oldest Little Flock boys were coming too. Tre counted ten people, not counting himself and Skylin, and all had been injured. He wasn't sure how successful this small group would be against the hardened warriors, who greatly outnumbered them.

All the weapons had been gathered and inspected. The ones that needed to be fixed were put aside. There were two long spears from the dead raiders in the ready pile, and each member of the rescue mission picked out a weapon. They decided to leave the following morning to give everyone a second day to rest and recover from their injuries. The first day of travel would take them to where the stream from the purple mountains joined the river. Rin knew the place well; it was where she had found Tre. The second day would bring them close to the raiders' compound. When Rin had escaped, she ran all night to reach the river. She knew the rescue team would need to keep that pace.

Rin explained to the rescue team that, once they were out of the mountains, the land became flat but many large rocks were scattered on the ground. It was important that everyone knew as much detail as possible to succeed in freeing Moon and the two women. They should be able to make it to the compound the second day. They would hide, wait out the night, and then attack just before daylight. She knew where the captives were held, and she and Axe would free them. Dellis, Little Flock, and the men would fight the lowlanders. They would attack the same way the raiders did on their village. At dawn, using fire arrows, they would set the large round communal building where everyone slept on fire. When the lowlanders ran out of the burning building, the villagers would be waiting for them. Rin warned the rescue team, "Watch out for the women. They are as mean and cruel as the men. Don't be fooled by them." From the horror in her voice everyone knew she had been cruelly treated by the women too.

Rin pulled Tre aside and made him promise. "If we can't get Moon out or if I get captured again, you must kill us. If not we will be slowly tortured to death or fed alive to their wolf pack. You would not believe the things I've seen them do to the prisoners. Promise me." She grabbed Tre's shoulders and shook them. He could only nod his head as he stared at her. His mouth opened, but no sound came out. He could not verbally make such a terrible promise to his mother, but he knew she was right.

The small rescue party left early in the morning. Rin wore a pair of Tre's tattered pants and had Windel's old sword tied with a piece of rope around her waist. She was shabbily dressed, and the wounds on her face and arms were swollen and red, but Tre was very proud of her. Rin was brave and strong and smart. Dellis and Axe led the men and boys of Little Flock. Tre knew the small rescue team of only twelve people could not defeat the fierce warriors that greatly outnumbered them. He tried to reason with Rin, but she turned away saying no matter the odds, they were going. No longer would they cower against the evil lowlanders.

When the rescue party reached the old hut outside the village, Tre took Skylin aside. He asked her to go to

Fairland and see if Queen Laurel would send help. Tre knew the secret army Mallrok had formed would even the odds against the rescue party. He walked with Skylin to where Cerra waited and saw Koda perched in the tree from which he had guarded Tre for so long. Tre looked at the two animals and said, "Keep her safe." He had grown fond of the girl he had once disliked and thought of as rude and strange. Skylin followed Cerra back through the dark forest, then stopped, turned, and yelled to her twin, "Be careful, brother, until I get back to protect you." He heard her laughter as she disappeared into the dark of the forest. Tre smiled. His sister had not changed, but he realized that he had.

By nightfall the small group had made camp where the purple mountain stream and river met. The place brought back memories for Rin, and she looked at Tre. How quickly he had grown into a young man from the small boy she rescued. She smiled with pride. The rescue team was exhausted after one day of travel, and Tre worried that the trip was too much for them. But as tired and hurt as they were, their determination to get back those taken captive was greater. Dellis and Axe leaned against a tree eating their day's ration of bread and cheese. They knew water would be an issue once they left the river and entered the dry land below.

Tre volunteered to take first guard. He wasn't as tired as the others and had no wounds to heal. Rin had instructed everyone to stay in a single line tomorrow. She didn't want to create a dust trail and signal their presence. "Stay close to the rocks as much as possible, and keep the horse last in line." The horse belonged to one of the raiders that had been killed, and it would be used to carry anyone unable to walk on their return. Rin warned everyone, "Don't get close to the flat-leafed plants. They look harmless but have sharp needles with hooked ends, and you can't get them out unless you cut them out."

Tre stood watch at the river's edge, leaning on his staff. Dellis finished washing his hands in the river, and, shaking them dry, walked over to Tre. "You sure have changed. You don't even look like your old self, and that sister of yours." Dellis shook his head as if it would help him understand all the changes that had taken place. "It's strange to think that you're not Rin's son and come from a place no one knew about and have a twin sister."

"Tell me." Tre laughed at Dellis's confusion and admitted, "I hardly know myself anymore. My whole life has been turned upside down."

Dellis looked from Tre's new clothes to his and the other villagers' ragged attire. "Looks like it turned out for the best," he said and yawned. "I better get some sleep. Another long day awaits tomorrow." Tre wanted to discuss his concerns about the rescue attempt with Dellis, but he knew it would not change anything.

*   *   *

It was dark when Skylin arrived at Old Nanny's house. With Cerra in the lead, she only stopped once to rest on her return. She looked inside the window; it was dark and empty. She turned away and headed toward the castle. It felt good to stay in the open, not having to hide from Kross any longer. Still, the large castle built into the side of the mountain did not feel like home. She felt uneasy at the vastness of it. Or was it too luxurious? She wasn't sure. Old Nanny's house was her home. It was close to the trees where she had spent many hours tramping and hunting with Cerra. She reached the town square; it was dark. The only light came from the windows of homes, creating a soft, warm glow. Koda must have flown ahead, because when Skylin turned on the path that led to the castle, Queen Laurel and Mallrok were waiting at the gate.

Queen Laurel took her hand and led her into a large room with chairs facing a crackling fireplace. Skylin hurried to the fire to warm her hands, glad to escape the frigid air outside. Her mother and Mallrok sat down in the chairs, anxious to hear about what had happened. She turned around and hurriedly told them about the raid by the lowlanders, how the village burned to the ground, and about the people hurt and killed and the two women and girl taken prisoner. Skylin sat down, took her mother's hand, and said, "Rin is leading rescue, but the number of men is small. Tre is going with them and needs our help. Will you send the army that overthrew Kross to help him? Please." She begged for her brother.

Queen Laurel and Mallrok exchanged looks. "I can only ask the men, not order them to risk their lives. Until Tre came home, no one had any idea there was a way out of the valley," said the queen. She turned to Mallrok and said, "Send word to all the men. There will be a special meeting in the town square tomorrow morning. We can put the platform Kross built to use."

Mallrok stood and bowed. "Yes, my queen." Then he left the room.

"Oh Mother, it was horrible to see the burnt village and all those people hurt. They have lost everything: their homes, their animals, and their food for the winter." Skylin leaned against her mother, exhausted.

Queen Laurel put her arm around Skylin and led her daughter into the large cooking room, where Old Nanny waited. "First some food, and then to bed. Tomorrow we will see what can be done to help Tre." The queen watched as Skylin collapsed into a chair at the table, and Old Nanny placed warm broth and bread for her to eat.

The next morning all the men were gathering around the large wooden platform when Queen Laurel, Mallrok, and Skylin arrived. Mallrok helped the queen up the steps and to the middle of the platform. He stood behind her, ever vigilant. Cheers rose from the men crowded around the platform. The queen stepped forward and looked at them. "Brave men of Fairland, I am so proud of you. You endured years of cruelty at the hands of Kross and still had the courage to overthrow him." She paused and then continued. "There is another battle we are being asked to fight. Long ago Fairland was open to the outside. We traded with the people of the mountains and lowlands. For many years we all got along, but then something happened to cause the lowlanders to raid and steal from us. The mountain people tried to help but were overpowered by the lowlanders and went into hiding in the mountains. To protect us, our elders sealed off the entrance to Fairland. This stopped the raids, but it also sealed us in. Being shut off from the outside didn't stop evil from getting in. Kross was one of our finest young men, and look what happened when he became jealous of his brother, King Naveen. The lowlanders raided the mountain village where Tre grew up, killing and hurting those who cared for him as their own. They have taken women captive to be their slaves. The men from the village who are able are on their way to rescue the women. The rescue team is greatly outnumbered, and Tre has sent word asking for our help. It is up to you to decide. Do we help the mountain people or not? It is not an easy decision to go into battle with the vicious lowlanders. The choice is yours."

*   *   *

Rin, Tre, and Dellis crept as close as they dared to the lowlanders' compound. Rin warned them to be as quiet as possible; the lowlanders kept large wolf like creatures penned inside the compound. The lowlanders starved the wolves, and when someone tried to escape or broke the rules, they would set the pack on the prisoner. Tre was relieved the slight breeze in the air was coming toward them. He feared the wolves might get the rescue party's scent and warn the lowlanders of their attack. Rin pointed to a high fenced area. "Throw the meat in there, and let's hope the sleeping herbs work before you start the fire arrows." Dellis nodded that he understood.

Plans were completed. Rin and Axe would go to the prisoner cage and free Moon and the women. Cary, one of Little Flock's older boys, would use his bow to shoot fire arrows into the large round building. Tre knew Cary would not miss. He had watched Cary during practices, and Cary rarely missed a target. Dellis would position the men around the compound to fight the warriors as they rushed from the burning building. The white painted stripes on Rin's face glowed eerily in the dark. She and Axe had painted their faces like the warriors but used white for their stripes. Her stripes were for her parents who had been killed many years ago by the raiders. Axe had expressed that his stripes were for Windel. Axe had watched over the small boy like an older brother and had cried in anguish when he was killed by Tulac. Rin still had Windel's sword tied to her side, and Axe carried a large warrior spear.

Tre was last in line as Rin, Dellis, and Axe crept back to where the others were waiting for first light to put their plan into action. Rin sat on the ground next to Tre, leaned close, and whispered, "Remember your promise. Do not let Moon or the other prisoners live if we can't get them out." Tre knew Rin would never leave this place alive unless she was able to free Moon and the other women.

He glanced up at the half moon, most of its light blocked by slow-moving clouds. The clouds helped hide the party's presence. Tre waited and wondered about the large round building the lowlanders slept in. He had never seen any other buildings like it. Was it for protection from the wolf pack they kept in the compound?

Tre wished that Skylin had returned by now. He missed his twin's confidence. Going into battle was not something she feared. But with Cerra at her side, she wouldn't have much to fear. Day's light was only a few hours away. If Skylin was not successful in bringing help, they would be greatly outnumbered. Tre looked around at the small group and was filled with pride at their courage to take on an enemy as fierce as the lowlanders.

Chapter 10

The night sky was starting to lighten. The men gathered in a low huddle around Rin. She assured them this would be their final fight for freedom. It was time to get even for all the years of raids, killing, and cruelty. There was no turning back, and they would fight to end this evil.

Tre stared at his mother in awe, marveling at her courage. Rin went over everyone's assigned task one last time. There could be no hesitation once they entered the lowlanders' compound. Their lives depended on their plan succeeding. Two of the men would throw the meat pieces to the wolf pack. Dellis had arrows wrapped in grease soaked rags to be set on fire and shoot into the roof of the large round building. Rin and Axe would go directly to the prisoners' cage and free them. Little Flock and the other men would take positions at the door of the building to "greet" the lowlanders when they ran from the flames. Rin's emphasis on "greet" caused a murmur from Little Flock as they gripped their weapons and whispered the various ways they would greet the unsuspecting raiders.

Tre looked back toward the purple mountains hoping to see his sister. If Skylin wasn't successful and returned without help, it would be a fatal fight for the villagers. Could he keep his promise to his mother, worried Tre. Of course Rin was right, but could he really kill her or Moon?

He knew for sure he would fight to his death to protect them.

"It's time," Dellis whispered to the brave villagers. "Make sure the horse is secure," he said to the boy assigned to stay with the animal. "We may need him on the trip home."

Slowly the rescue party crept forward, careful to make no sound that would alert the wolves in the pen. Rin left the group and headed toward the wooden cage that held the prisoners. Axe followed close behind, their two shadows blending into one. The two men carrying a sack of meat quietly moved to the high-fenced pen, their soft moccasins making no sound. Dellis, Tre, and Little Flock edged around the building where the lowlanders slept.

Tre watched as his mother made her way to the prisoner cage. He turned to follow her, wanting to protect her, when he heard whining sounds from the high-fenced pen. The wolves had smelled the meat, and then loud growls began as the animals fought over it. Dellis lit the arrows on fire from a piece of burning wood he carried from the campsite. Tre hoped there would be enough time for the fire to take hold before the fighting wolves woke the warriors. Cary's aim was true, and the arrows hit the roof. The building quickly caught fire, lighting the compound area in an eerie glow. Little Flock was in its assigned places with weapons ready when the lowlanders ran out. Tre heard shouting from inside the burning building, but he could not understand the words. He pulled his knife from his belt and wished his twin was at his side.

Rin and Axe reached the caged area where the prisoners were held. From inside she could hear someone crying. She swung Windel's old sword, hitting the ropes that held the wooden slats of the cage together. Axe made a grunting noise and pointed with his spear for Rin to hit the ropes again. She put all of her strength behind the next swing, hitting the ropes with enough force to cut them apart. Axe sprang forward and started pulling the slats apart to make an opening for the women to escape. Rin ran to the cage yelling, "Moon. Moon. We came for you."

The young girl appeared at the side of the cage, reached her hand through the slats, and grabbed Rin's arm. "Rin!" Moon cried out in relief.

"Go get the others; we must hurry," Rin said. Time was critical as she watched the roof of the building catch fire.

The two village women staggered forward; one supported the other, who was barely able to walk. It was the butcher's wife, and her leg was broken. Axe reached through the opening in the cage and lifted each woman out. He picked up the butcher's wife and grunted, motioning with his head for the others to follow him as he ran into the darkness. Rin grabbed Moon by the hand and ran after Axe, looking back to make sure the other woman was keeping up. They reached the place where the horse was tied, and Axe sat the butcher's wife on the horse's back.

"Take them back the way we came. Don't stop for anything—no matter what you hear." Rin grabbed the young boy guarding the horse by the shoulders, making sure he understood. "Go!" she yelled and then hit the horse on its rump. Rin and Axe made sure Moon and the other woman ran after the horse before they turned and raced toward the burning building where the escaping lowlanders were now fighting Little Flock and the village men.

Flames from the building were burning Tre's eyes, and the smoke made it hard to breathe. He had knocked out two of the escaping lowlanders with his staff, but the others were running out faster than the small rescue party could keep up with. The warriors were armed with spears and knives, their bow and arrows useless in a close fight. A woman ran screaming from the building with her clothes in flames. Tre watched in shock at the horrible sight.

Shouts came from the animal pen as someone yelled, "Stop them—don't let them get out." A high-pitched yelping began. It seemed one of the wolves was hurt. The two village men were trying their best to keep the snarling beasts in the pen. Tre was fighting his own battle with one of the escaped warriors when another ran up behind him with his knife pulled back, ready to throw. Tre knew he could not stop them both from killing him. A long spear flew by his shoulder and hit the closest warrior in the chest. The warrior suddenly stopped his attack on Tre and slumped to the ground.

"Great throw, Axe," Rin shouted as the two ran to join the fight. Axe pulled his spear from the dead warrior and then turned to face another enraged warrior running from the fire-engulfed building.

There were two warriors for each Little Flock boy, but the boys fought hard, fueled by their determination for justice. Rin was cornered by an enraged lowland woman with a long knife, viciously slashing back and forth, trying her hardest to cut Rin. Smoke curled from the woman's long black hair, making her look like some fire demon. Rin jumped to the side as she watched the crazed woman, waiting for a chance to swing Windel's sword. Tre started to help Rin when he saw them coming. The wolves had escaped in spite of the village men's efforts, and they were heading toward him. Their snarling mouths were dripping with whitish foam and baring huge pointed teeth. They had long legs, matted gray hair, and were ferociously hungry. One of the pack leaped directly at Tre. He swung the long staff and hit the beast in midair. The wolf tumbled to the ground, its neck broken.

Dellis started yelling for Little Flock to pull back and form a circle to defend against the increasing number of lowlanders. Tre knew the chance of success was diminishing as the wolfish beasts joined the fight and the warriors' numbers increased. Tre turned to help Rin as she fought the shrieking woman. He didn't see a warrior run from behind the building. The lowlander's knife was raised, ready to stab Tre in the back. Rin glanced up and saw the warrior closing the distance to Tre. She screamed a warning, but with all the racket and noise, Tre didn't hear her.

A high-pitched screech drowned out all other sounds. It was so loud that even the wolves stopped their attack. The sound hurt Tre's ears, and he turned around to see the warrior behind him with knife raised. The warrior glared in hatred at Tre, ready to kill him, when two huge, clawed feet lifted the warrior off the ground. Sharp talons pierced the warrior's neck as he was carried high in the air and then dropped into the burning building. "Koda," Tre shouted, lifting his staff to thank the large owl, and then ran to help his mother. Koda made a circle and then dived down and grabbed another warrior, carried him high, and dropped him in the fire.

The lowlanders and the wolves had Dellis and Little Flock surrounded, and the fighting was fierce. A large yellow mountain cat sprang forward and roared loudly. "Cerra this way," Tre yelled and ran toward the wolf pack. Cerra came up beside Tre and leaped into the middle of the ferocious animals. With two large swipes of his massive paws he sent one of the wolves limping away, howling in pain. The snarling wolf pack turned and started to surround Cerra. Tre tried to hit the wolves with his staff, but they were fast, jumping out of his way and trying to sink their fangs into Cerra. The largest wolf turned and leaped at Tre. Tre was slow to bring around his staff to block the attack when a knife with a carved wooden handle landed in the middle of the beast's head. The large wolf fell to the ground with mouth gaped open and tongue hanging out. Skylin ran up and shouted, "You couldn't wait for me, brother?"

"You should have gotten here sooner," Tre shouted back grinning widely.

Shouts of relief came from Little Flock and the village men as the Fairland army came rushing in to join the fight. Now the lowlanders were outnumbered. Tre and Skylin teamed with Cerra to kill the vicious wolves. The fighting ended when the remaining lowlanders tried to run away but were blocked by the Fairland army.

"Tulak!" Rin screamed and yelled more words Tre did not understand. In the lowland language, Rin issued a challenge to the evil leader. The large warrior turned at his name being called and glared, trying to identify his challenger. When he recognized Rin, he pointed his finger, laughed, and yelled back at her. From the look on Rin's face, Tre knew the warrior leader was taunting her.

With Windel's sword held high, she ran at him, her painted face as fierce as his. Tulak laughed in the same callous way he did when he killed Windel. Rin screamed out loud as she charged the ruthless lowland leader. Tulak smirked at her and readied his spear to throw at the charging Rin, when a spear identical to his plunged deeply into his chest. Tulac stumbled and grabbed at the spear embedded in his heart, and then he slumped to the ground. Axe ran up beside Rin, grunted, and pointed to the stripes on his face and then at Tulak. He had his vengeance for Windel, his small friend who he had carried around on his shoulders.

Rin glared as she looked down at the dead leader and said to Axe, "Throw him in the fire," and pointed at the burning building. "Dellis, burn everything. Don't leave one piece of wood. This place must vanish forever." Axe started tearing down the cage where the prisoners were held and threw the wood into the fire. Everyone joined in until all signs of the compound had been devoured by flames. Skylin led the wounded villagers to the side where their injuries were washed and treated.

The leader of the army walked up to Tre and asked, "What should we do with the rest of the lowlanders?" He pointed to one end of the compound where the Fairland army had a small group of captives surrounded. Tre counted twelve women and children huddled together in fear. He looked around at all the injured being treated for their wounds. Tre went over to Rin and led her to where the captives were held. "Mother, will you tell them we will let them live, but they have to leave this land and never return?" Tre pointed to the edge of the desert land. "Tell them to go to those far mountains, and if they ever return they will be killed." Rin nodded and walked over to the cowered group, no longer the horrible monsters of her nightmares. In their language Rin repeated Tre's orders and pointed toward the mountains at the far end of the desert floor. The Fairland army parted to allow the prisoners to escape. The defeated lowlanders rushed out of the smoking compound and scurried away in to the desert. Tre asked the leader to post a watch to make sure they did not turn back.

With all traces of the compound destroyed and the wounded treated, Dellis lead the rescue party back toward the river. The return trip was slower with the wounded and exhausted villagers, but still jubilant. Tre and Skylin stopped for one last look at the flat, dusty land before starting up the hilly slope. Cerra and Koda waited nearby. "Finally the raids and killings are over," Tre said. Then he turned to Skylin. "Thank you again for saving me. If you hadn't shown up when you did, well, none of us would be alive."

Skylin grinned and said, "Saving you is becoming a habit. Having a 'younger' brother is a pain." Then she laughed in her annoying way, which didn't annoy him anymore. Skylin turned to Tre, her tone serious. "You should not have let them go. You don't set your enemies free."

Tre shook his head at her words and had no response. Finally he said, "Come on. Let's go home."

It was evening when the tired group reached the campsite where the rivers met. Tre looked at the river and thought it would always be a special place for Rin and him. Their beginning was here. As Tre stepped into camp, a young girl with long brown hair ran to him and flung her arms around his neck. "I knew you would come for me. I just knew it in my heart." Moon hugged him tight.

"Moon, mother would be lost without her little bird to sing with," Tre replied as he tried to loosen her tight hold on his neck.

She leaned back, looked at him, and asked, "Would you be lost too?"

Tre stammered, not sure what to say, when Skylin walked over and slapped him on the shoulder and said, "Yeah would you be lost too, brother?" She laughed and walked to where Rin and Dellis sat at the river's edge.

She told them, "We'll be leaving for Fairland in the morning. I have a message from Queen Laurel for you and your village. Don't worry about food for the winter. Fairland has plenty, and if you want to move to the meadow on the other side of the river, Fairland will help you build new homes."

Rin stood up, took Skylin's hand, and almost cried as she said, "Thank the queen for me. You saved us."

Skylin leaned close to Rin and said, "One more thing." She whispered in Rin's ear.

Rin smiled and said, "Tell the queen, she is welcome."

Tre decided to stay with Rin and the villagers to help them get safely home and would stay until they moved to the grassy meadow. He was excited and told Rin it would be a great place to grow crops and raise livestock. It would be close to Fairland, so he could visit often. Finally his curiosity could not be contained, and he asked Rin, "What did Skylin whisper to you?"

Rin stopped walking and looked at Tre. She placed her hands on the side of his face and smiled. "Queen Laurel said, 'Thank you for saving and taking care of *our* son.'"

The Twins of Fairland

Part 3

The Magic

Chapter 11

Trey halted the big red horse and, from his vantage point on the mountain trail, sat looking down at the new village. The homes for the mountain people had been finished. Walls stood for shops for the butcher and the blacksmith, and once the roofs were added they would be complete. The villagers had dismantled and moved the bakery since it was spared from the fire. It was in the first building erected in the large meadow. Smoke curled from the bakery's chimney. Rin and Moon did the all of the baking and cooking for the villagers, and this freed everyone to work on their homes and shops.

After the battle with the lowlanders, the rescuers returned to their burnt village. They treated the wounded and made plans to move to the large meadow. Tre showed the way there, but the men decided the fallen-tree bridge would be too dangerous for the women and children to cross, and they would not be able to carry their few salvaged belongings over the dangerous tree bridge. Lower down the mountainside the river curved and narrowed, and Axe and Dellis built a large wooden raft to ferry the villagers and their belongings across. The raft also allowed the men to cross back to hunt game in the mountains. Queen Laurel kept her word, and when the villagers arrived in the meadow, food, blankets, and tools were waiting to help them survive the coming winter. The winter months were milder in the meadow, and the villagers did not have to endure the harsh freezing temperatures on the high mountain slopes.

After months of hard work, the new village was proof of the resilience of the mountain people. Tre had labored many long hours alongside his friends to help rebuild their homes and their lives. The memories and scars would always be there, but the villagers were happy living in the meadow and gaining new friends in Fairland. The constant threat of the lowlanders was left in the past as they moved forward.

Tre had gone with Axe back to the burnt village one final time to search for the cows and chickens but found no signs of the animals. The walls of the small butcher shop were still standing, and Tre looked at the gouges in the back door where he had learned to throw his knife. The old hut that had been his home had finally given way to the harsh weather and lay collapsed on the ground.

Mallrok had taken Queen Laurel to the place where Fairland had been sealed many years ago. The queen ordered the entrance to be opened, and the men from town spent many days moving large rocks. With the way into Fairland open once again, the queen had been able to keep her promise to Rin and deliver the needed supplies to the villagers. When the people of Fairland learned there was a way out of the hidden valley, they were excited at the opportunity to see the land beyond the tall purple mountains. There had been many changes in Fairland with Queen Laurel again on the throne. With the wicked Kross gone, the people were happy and now greeted each other with smiles and laughter and no longer hid in their homes behind locked doors and closed windows. The town square was once again used for games and dancing. Tre and Skylin became heroes, and everyone greeted them. It was so different from how Skylin had been avoided before. The twins' reputations increased each time the battle with the lowlanders was retold and their heroics grew. Skylin reveled in the notoriety, but Tre would rather it be forgotten.

Tre and Skylin had grown close in the years since their first meeting, and what a meeting it had been, with Tre scared witless and Skylin enjoying his distress. Skylin taught Tre how to ride a horse. Tre fell off more times than he wanted, but he finally mastered the skill. Knees tight and moving with the horse's gait, now he could almost keep up with his sister. Thankfully he was a fast learner. Tre's horse was a large chestnut with a white patch on his forehead. Skylin named him Patch, but Tre shortened it to Pat, quickly becoming attached to the large animal. Skylin's horse was a smoky gray she called Wind. And she rode like the wind, as fast as the horse could run, with her long blonde hair flying behind. The twins' favorite pastime was riding across the long valley of Fairland, enjoying many hours together.

As Pat trotted down the trail to the village, Tre noticed something strange. An old woman wrapped in a woven blanket was camped outside the bakery. Two young boys with their dark hair in braids sat around the campsite. The three strangers stopped what they were doing to stare at Tre. He frowned as he took in their appearance; they did not look like mountain people.

Tre dismounted and tied Pat's reins to a post outside the bakery. He saw Dellis carrying wood for one of the buildings and hurried over to help. When the sturdy planks were stacked on the ground, the two friends clasped hands in greeting. Tre asked Dellis about the old woman and the two boys and where they came from. Dellis told him they wandered up to the river crossing and waited for the raft to come across. Since they looked to be starving and no one could understand her, the men ferried them across the river and brought them to Rin.

Rin said to feed them and let them stay in the village until the village council decided what to do about them. The old woman communicates with Rin in a language close to the lowlanders. She told Rin they came from beyond the mountains, but nothing more. The boys stay close to the old woman and don't join the other children in play. Tre felt uneasy as he looked at the strangers, but did not mention it.

Tre asked Dellis how everything was going, and Dellis said the homes were finished and the shops only needed roofs. Dellis was proud at what had been accomplished and had become a capable leader. He said when spring arrived everyone would be able to work the land to get it ready for planting. With seeds and instruction from Fairland, the villagers would be able to grow their own crops.

Tre left Dellis to his work and went to find Rin in the bakery. She stopped mixing a batch of dough when she saw him enter. With a smile on her face and light in her eyes she welcomed her son, always the proud mother. Rin updated Tre on the latest happenings, causing him to laugh at the catastrophe of Axe and a startled skunk. Tre asked Rin about the strangers. Rin replied that the council would decide what to do about them, but she could not let the old woman and the two young boys starve. The old woman offered to weave the wild grasses into baskets and mats if she and her two grandsons could stay. Rin added, "They haven't caused any trouble and keep to themselves." Apparently Rin was not concerned about them, and the council's decision would settle the matter.

Tre went outside to check on Pat but noticed the butcher working in his new shop and walked over. They greeted each other with the mountain salute, hands grasped and arms held tight at the elbows. Growing up in the mountain village, Tre had grown close to the stout man. The butcher and his wife did not have children, and he took a special interest in Tre. The old knife was still Tre's favorite treasure. Tre asked the butcher about his wife's recovery after being taken captive by the lowlanders. The butcher replied, "Thanks to Rin, her leg has mended and she can now walk without a stick." Appreciation lined his face.

Tre wandered back into the bakery and saw Moon busy cooking. When she noticed Tre, she quickly took off her apron and hurried out to greet him. In the past year Moon had grown from the gangly girl that followed Little Flock around into a pretty brown-eyed young woman. She shyly asked Tre if he would like something to eat. The sun was high in the sky, and he was getting hungry. "That sounds great," Tre replied. Moon carried a large bowl of venison stew and set it down on the long wooden table. "Mmm, this is delicious. You're a good cook, Moon," he said as he took a second large spoonful. Moon blushed.

The winter hunting had been good, and with the grain and food from Fairland, the villagers look healthier than ever before, no longer starving on the high mountain slope. Tre could still remember when he and Rin would have to share a few scraps of meat and bread when the supplies ran low. Tre finished his stew and went to find Rin. "Mother, do you need anything before I leave?" he asked.

She answered, "We have enough food and grain for a while." Rin walked Tre to the door and watched as he jumped on Pat's back and galloped away. He turned and waved to his mother and experienced an uneasy feeling, not sure if he should leave.

Tre had reached the new road into Fairland when Skylin galloped up on Wind, looking disheveled. "Why did you take off without telling me?" she yelled at him and then ranted, "Mother is trying to make me learn to cook and run the household staff. Old Nanny needs help, but it's not me."

Tre knew household duties and Skylin did not mix and laughed to himself. "There are plenty of women in town that can help Old Nanny. Just ask next time you're there. Besides, I told you yesterday that I needed to check on Rin." Tre tried to reason with his sister, but at times there was no reasoning with Skylin.

The twins rode to the corral behind the castle. They rubbed down, fed, and watered the horses. As they walked to the castle, Skylin looked up and said, "I'm still not comfortable here. It's too closed in."

Tre stopped and looked at the large rock fortress. "You saw where I grew up. This place is just the opposite. We were lucky not to starve or freeze to death in the winter," he said. As the twins entered the castle, they were so engrossed in their discussion that they did not see Queen Laurel and Mallrok in a small side room intently talking.

The twins went directly to the large cooking room to get a piece of cake and a mug of milk. It had become a habit after their rides. Skylin didn't want to learn to cook, but she took great pleasure in food. She could out-eat most men. Axe was the only one who could match her bite for bite. As they sat down at the table, anxious to enjoy their treat, Old Nanny shuffled in, "Where have you two been?" she exclaimed, her brogue prominent. "Now is not the time to go off and not tell anyone!" She fiercely shook the big wooden ladle in her hand at them.

From the frown on her wrinkled face, the twins could tell something was worrying her. "What's wrong?" they asked in unison.

"Haven't you heard? Cattle and grain from the barns have started disappearing, and Mallrok is putting guards out tonight." Old Nanny shook her head.

Skylin gulped her milk and said, "How much grain is missing, and who is taking it?" Stealing in Fairland was not a common event.

"Enough to cause worry, especially with sending food to help Rin's people," Old Nanny answered.

Tre came to the defense of his mother. "As soon as spring comes, the villagers can plant their own crops and start raising their own animals. I don't think they are stealing from Fairland."

"Ah, no. It's not them," Old Nanny said, without explaining further.

"Then who is doing it?" Tre asked, but Old Nanny didn't answer as she turned away and slowly made her way from the room.

Skylin drummed the table with her fingers as she waited for Tre to finish his cake. After clearing the table of their dishes, the twins hurried to find Queen Laurel. Mallrok was leaving when they entered the small room where their mother sat. "Mother, what is going on?" Skylin asked as she hurried over.

Queen Laurel turned to face her children, looking concerned. "We're not sure. Mallrok is going to investigate."

"Should we go with him?" Skylin said as she watched the tall, robed man walk down the hall.

"No," the queen quickly replied with fear in her voice. "We will wait for Mallrok to return."

Chapter 12

Tre stayed in the castle the rest of the day and all of the next, anxiously waiting for Mallrok to return. He was amazed to see how busy Queen Laurel was in running Fairland. There were so many things to deal with, but she was fair and patient with everyone. "Where did Mallrok go?" Tre asked his mother. They were in the castle's large library. It was Tre's favorite room in the castle, like the cooking room was Skylin's.

Skylin entered the room and heard her mother reply to Tre's question, "To the far end of the valley, where the mountains begin."

Skylin walked up and said, "Where they hid you in the cabin? I went there once to see it for myself. It's a long way, and there is nothing back there except rock ledges and old caves. Cerra wasn't happy there, so I didn't stay long." The queen looked surprised at Skylin's admission, but stayed silent.

On the third day Mallrok finally returned to the castle and quickly called a meeting with Queen Laurel and the leaders of Fairland. As Skylin and Tre tried to enter the large room where everyone was gathering, Mallrok blocked their way. Skylin faced Mallrok with her hands on her hips, demanding to be let in. Tre was hesitant to challenge Mallrok so blatantly and looked toward his mother. Queen

Laurel saw what was happening at the doorway. She hesitated for a moment and then motioned for Mallrok to let the twins enter. Mallrok nodded and moved aside.

When everyone was seated around the long table, Mallrok stood up and stunned the group with a startling revelation. "At the far end of the valley where the mountains begin, there are hidden passageways that go down inside the mountains to large caves. Many years ago the inhabitants that lived in the mountains, called slags, would raid Fairland for food. They would always raid at night. These raids led to fierce battles between Fairland and the slags, with both sides suffering great losses. Finally, it was agreed that the mountains beyond the valley would belong to the slags and their domain would be the caves inside the mountains. They are night creatures accustomed to darkness from years of living in the deep caves.

"I've come from a meeting with their mystic leader, and this is what I have learned: When Kross went into hiding, he hid in the caves, which is why no one could find him. Somehow he learned of the slags and made an agreement to supply them with food to allow him to stay hidden and build his army. The food supplies stopped when Kross was killed, so now Haaman, the slags' mystic leader, is demanding their monthly allotment or they will continue to raid and pillage Fairland."

"The slags threatened Fairland?" Queen Laurel gasped but did not look as shocked as everyone else seated around the table. The queen and Mallrok must have known who was raiding the grain barns. "Did you tell them Kross is dead?" the queen asked.

Mallrok responded, "Haaman doesn't care. He said they made a treaty with Fairland, and he is demanding payment."

"This is a problem." Queen Laurel looked concerned.

"There is more, the slags are armed with weapons Kross gave them, and there's another issue." Mallrok looked at the queen, silently nodded his head, and said, "The old ones have passed down their magic, and Haaman said he would use his powers to protect the slags. I also saw strange-looking animals hiding in the caves."

Everyone at the table was too stunned to speak, trying to make sense of what they heard: Haaman, a mystic leader, old magic passed down, slags all this time living in the mountain caves. Queen Laurel thanked Mallrok for his report and told the leaders they must come up with a plan to protect the grain barns and cattle from further raids. Then the queen stood up and left the room, signaling the meeting was over. After the queen left, Mallrok and the leaders began to discuss ways to protect Fairland.

The twins followed their mother from the room since they were not included in the planning. "What is the old magic, and how does Mallrok know all these things?" they asked, still dazed from Mallrok's shocking revelation.

The queen turned, looked at the twins, and paused to gather her thoughts before she replied. "A long time ago when Fairland was called farland, it was a time when the lowlanders and farlanders were ruled by mystic leaders with magical powers. The slags were part of farland but always stayed inside the mountains. Through the years the old powers have died out, but apparently some of them have been passed down through the guard line. Now, I need to attend to some matters." The queen turned and walked away.

Tre was alarmed. He knew Mallrok was different and had secrets. He seemed to know all about the ancient magic. *At one time was he, or is he still, a mystic with powers?* wondered Tre. What about Cerra and Koda and his twin's uncanny ability to communicate with them? Is Skylin part of the old guard line? These thoughts tumbled around in Tre's head. He looked at his twin and loudly exclaimed, "What should we do?"

Skylin was not concerned. "Our army will protect us. I'm not sure about Haaman's mystic powers or if there are others like him." She looked at Tre and then admitted, "I've heard the stories from Old Nanny, but I never thought they were true. You know how Old Nanny is always babbling about something."

Tre replied, "Great, more scary things to worry about." *Could the old tales be real?* he wondered.

Tre and Skylin were restless after hearing Mallrok's story of the slags, the old ways, and the magic. Since they had not been included in the meeting to protect the barns, they decided to watch for the night raiders themselves. At dusk they dressed in dark clothing and snuck out of the castle. They climbed the hillside and hid in the tree line to keep watch on the barn that was closest to town. Skylin was fidgety at having to be quiet and sit still. She was driving Tre crazy with her constant moving around and sighing. Stealth was not part of her makeup.

It was the darkest part of the night when Cerra gave a low growl. The twins could not see anything in the black mist, so they decided to light the torches they had placed around the barn earlier in the day. Tre ran along one side of the large barn and Skylin the other, both lighting the torches with a burning stick. They tended a small fire during the night, only adding one piece of wood at a time to keep it burning. As soon as the torches were lit, the barn was illuminated from outside. They heard muffled noises coming from inside the barn. Then suddenly high-pitched shrieks filled the air.

Tre and Skylin raced around their side of the large barn and met in the front, each holding a blazing torch. They pulled open the wide doors and stood side by side in the middle of the opening. From the light of the torches small creatures with whitish skin and long, skinny arms could be seen. They wore sacklike garments tied at the middle with ropes. The creatures scrambled away from the light, hiding large bug like eyes with their bony hands. Tre counted at least six of them, each dragging a sack they had been filling with grain.

The twins stood fixed in place, stunned at seeing the wraithlike creatures. Tre had never seen anything like them. They looked to be human but not entirely. The creatures backed away from the light, saw the twins blocking the doorway, and began snarling, revealing small pointy teeth. The twins inched closer together holding the torches high. Catching the twins by surprise, the creatures scurried to Tre's side of the barn. As they creatures raced by, one of them reached out and slashed Tre's leg with long razor-sharp nails. It happened so fast there was no time for him to move out of the way. The creatures escaped into the night, carrying their partially filled sacks.

"Those things belong in a bad dream," Skylin exclaimed. "They were here, and now they're gone." When Tre didn't answer, she turned and saw blood running down his leg. Tre stumbled backward in shock as blood gushed from deep gashes. Terror filled Skylin as she searched for something to bind around his leg to stop the bleeding. Hurriedly she pulled her knife from her belt, ripped apart a sack one of the creatures left behind, scattering grain all over the floor. She tightly wrapped the torn sack around Tre's leg and helped him to the side of the barn. "Stay here. I'll go get help," she ordered, but Tre didn't hear her as he slid to the floor, unconscious.

Skylin raced to the castle, her long legs flying. Two men were guarding the entrance who were not there when the twins snuck out at dusk. They saw someone running down the path to the castle screaming loudly and raised their weapons. When they recognized Skylin, they moved aside to allow her to enter. Skylin's screams for help filled the castle. Queen Laurel rushed out of her bedroom, tying her robe around the waist as she hurried down the hallway to meet her daughter. The queen was frightened because she has never heard Skylin scream like this. Skylin ran directly to her mother, her eyes filled with fear and uttered, "Tre is hurt. I tried to stop the bleeding, but the cuts are deep." Skylin was beside herself, wringing her hands and unable to stand still.

The queen held Skylin's hands in hers and asked, "Where is Tre?" Taking a deep breath, Skylin quickly told the queen about the raid and the creatures and Tre lying unconscious in the barn.

Queen Laurel hurried to the castle entrance and ordered the guards to find Tre and bring him to the castle. "Carry him to Old Nanny," the queen yelled as the guards ran down the path toward the barn.

Skylin paced back and forth while she waited with her mother, repeating over and over, "I had no idea those creatures were so dangerous. This is all my fault."

Old Nanny had her medicine bag sitting on the large table, ready to tend to Tre's wounds. "Don't worry young one, Tre is strong and healthy. It will take more than a slag to do him harm." Old Nanny reached out and pulled Skylin into her arms to comfort her as she did so many times before.

*   *   *

The next morning, Queen Laurel and Mallrok sat with Tre and Skylin around the large stone fireplace. Tre was in a chair with his bandaged leg propped up on cushions. Mallrok, anxious to hear about the raid, listened as the twins admitted what happened. The queen was upset with the slags for coming so close to town and with the twins for not telling her or Mallrok what they had planned. From the strained look on her face, Tre and Skylin realized how careless they had been, not understanding the menace they faced and treating the situation like a game. Worse, they had caused their mother unnecessary worry.

Mallrok told the queen, "It's hard to fight these creatures at night. The fire torches will help keep them away, but Haaman is not going to give up when there is food to take from Fairland."

Queen Laurel added, "They are getting braver to come all the way into town."

Mallrok stood up and admitted, "I'm sure the night torches won't deter them for long either." As he left, he looked at the twins and sternly warned, "You two stay out of trouble."

*   *   *

The next day, Trey hobbled to the library. He couldn't walk on his leg until the stitches Old Nanny had made to close his wounds healed, so he used his staff for support to get around the castle. Queen Laurel entered the large, book-filled room, and said, "I thought I would find you here. I came to see if you need anything."

Tre closed the book he was reading to ask his mother a question that had been bothering him. "Is Mallrok related to us?"

The queen paused for a moment then told Tre, "He is my uncle, but older. The age of my father's father and the last of the mystical guards of Fairland. His magic is not strong any longer, and that worries him with the slags causing trouble." Tre pondered this revelation; if Mallrok is his mother's uncle, then the twins were also related to him. He wasn't sure if this new knowledge gave him comfort or not.

After the queen left the room, Tre noticed an old, worn book leaning in the corner of a bookshelf. Using his staff for support, he limped over, picked it up, and carried it back to his chair. It took a while for Tre to interpret the words, and what he read caused him to wonder. It was an old legend, written in ancient script, of twins born to carry on the guard line as protectors of farland.

Tre couldn't wait for Skylin to return to the castle and show her what he had found. She had left early in the morning while he was still sleeping. Even with Mallrok's warning to stay out of trouble, he was sure she was out looking for signs the scary night creatures had returned. Skylin always went to bed after Tre and was up hours before him. Sleep was not one of her priorities; like Cerra, she was always on the prowl. Tre grinned. That pretty much summed up his twin.

Chapter 13

The old woman stopped weaving the basket to watch Moon enter the bakery, her beady eyes moving back and forth, always watching. The old woman sat and listened; she knew more than she let on. The two boys stayed close. Axe stopped working on the roof of the new butcher shop and watched the old woman. He frowned and wondered about the large blackbirds that now hung around her campsite. The old woman constantly muttered to herself and had started making bundles out of sticks and pieces of rope. She would wave her hands over the bundles, chanting unknown words. When she set a bundle on the ground, one of the big blackbirds would swoop down and fly off with it.

Axe motioned for Dellis to come over, and they both watched the strange things unfolding at the campsite. The old woman was very careful around Rin. She acted happy and thankful, smiling her toothless smile and nodding her head. She brought the mats and baskets she wove to Rin to use in the bakery. The old woman made colorful ties for Moon's hair and insisted that Moon let her braid her long brown hair with them. Axe grunted at Dellis and shook his head.

"I agree, but we don't know what she is up to, so we'll keep watching her," Dellis told his large friend.

* * *

Skylin finally returned to the castle, but she had not been out hunting the night creatures. She had rode to the meadow to tell Rin that Tre was okay, in case word reached Rin about the night creatures' raid and Tre getting hurt. Skylin still felt responsible for Tre's injury. She found him in the library and excitedly told him the latest news from the village. "Everyone has agreed to name the new village after Rin, since she led them to victory over the lowlanders. They decided to name the village and meadow Rinland." Tre was astonished, as he had not heard anything about naming the new village.

Skylin scooted her chair closer to her brother. With a worried look on her face, she said, "I am concerned about that old woman; she is not as harmless as Rin thinks, and those large blackbirds are messengers."

Tre asked, "How do you know they are messengers?"

"I can tell!" Skylin responded. She did not need to think about it; she just knew.

"Did you tell Rin?" Tre asked, again worried since his sister confirmed his suspicion about the old woman.

"No, she was busy, but Dellis and Axe are keeping close watch on the old woman now," Skylin replied.

"How is Dellis?" Tre questioned, watching for his sister's reaction. Skylin and Dellis were spending more time together, and she had begun making frequent trips to the meadow. Skylin had given Dellis a horse to ride, and they went riding when she visited. Dellis had been wounded during the lowlanders' raid on the mountain village, but over the long winter months and all the work involved to rebuild the village, his wounds had healed and he was fit and strong once again.

Skylin jumped up, intending to stomp out of the room, but Tre yelled, "Wait. I have something important to show you." She stopped at the doorway and turned, watching as Tre hobbled over to a table where an old, worn book rested. "Come here." He motioned. "I found this old book. It has a legend in it about the old times before Fairland." The book's cover was worn thin and as Tre carefully opened it, the pages crackled with age. "I can read most of it. Rin taught me to read when I was little." Tre carefully turned the page in awe. He thought of all the others before him who had held and read the old book.

Skylin didn't say anything, because when Old Nanny tried to teach her to read she had protested and made Old Nanny so miserable that the reading lessons did not last long. Skylin could read and write enough to get by. "Go ahead and read it," Skylin haughtily said, not wanting to admit she had no idea what the strange scribbling meant.

"It is an old scribe; the words are spelled a little different. It took me a while, but I figured it out like a riddle," Tre told her, but Skylin just stood there staring suspiciously at the old book.

Tre pointed to the page and haltingly translated.

> *When the ancient guards are no more,*
> *An old enemy will come forth to challenge the rule.*
> *Do not despair.*
> *The guard line will survive.*
> *Twin warriors shall lead their people to victory.*

"Strange isn't it?" Tre said.

"It's just some old myth like Old Nanny used to tell me." Skylin turned and walked out of the room, leaving Tre to his books. She didn't want him to see that she was troubled by the old myth. If Mallrok was Queen Laurel's uncle, then he was the twins' blood relative. She always knew she was different from the other children, more comfortable roaming the woods with Cerra and Koda than attending learning classes in town. She was never scared or concerned about her welfare, and Tre was different in his own way. He was more like their mother. He was smart and could do things she couldn't, such as figuring out that the old scribe. He could read all the books in the castle and understand things so easily. Skylin stomped away upset and unsure why.

It had been three days since Mallrok left the castle after hearing about the twins' encounter with the slags. Tre's leg was almost healed. He could stand on it without any pain. Old Nanny was an amazing healer. She had stitched up the gashes in his leg and then put a concoction she had made on the wounds. She said it was a healing poultice made from plants that grew in the mountains. Each day she would unwrap the cloth from around his leg, wash the wound, and apply a new poultice. She told him today was the last day he would need it.

As Tre sat at the table after Old Nanny rewrapped his leg, he thought of Rin and how she did her best to help the wounded mountain people. If she knew how to make the healing poultice, it would help the villagers. He would ask Old Nanny if she would teach Rin to make this medicine. It could make a difference as to whether someone survived an injury or not. Tre stood and slowly made his way back to his favorite room without the use of his staff.

The sun was high above when Tre heard sounds in the large hall. He had been looking through some of the old books, trying to learn more of Fairland's history. He closed the book and stood up when he recognized Mallrok's voice. Queen Laurel hurried to meet Mallrok and said, "You look tired. Let's go sit down." Mallrok followed the queen and sat down at the long table in the cooking room.

Tre walked behind and sat across from Mallrok. Old Nanny brought Mallrok a large mug of steaming broth. He held the mug with both hands and sipped its contents. "Thank you, Veerna." He sighed and looked ready to collapse. "It is not good news I bring. I met with Haaman, and he will not stop the raids until his demands are met. He said his people will starve. I was not aware that Kross had been giving the slags food and cattle all these years." Mallrok shook his head in disbelief.

The queen questioned, "What should we do? We may not have enough grain to make it until the next harvest, sending help to the mountain people and Kross depleting our barns without anyone knowing. The situation is serious." The big cooking room became quiet; neither knew how to solve the problem.

Queen Laurel's voice broke the silence. "How serious is the threat to Fairland? Do you think it will come to war with the slags?"

Mallrok responded, "It is very serious. Haaman would not back down. He demands payment and is ready for war."

The queen was troubled with Mallrok's news, and worry lined her face. The once prosperous Fairland would now have to ration what was left of last year's harvest or face starving, themselves. The queen said, "Call a meeting tomorrow with the leaders. Fairland must prepare." Mallrok nodded his head, his long gray beard brushing the table. He sat his empty mug down, slowly stood, and left the room.

Tre reached across the table and took hold of his mother's hand. He wanted to comfort her. "Everything will work out. Fairland will be okay," he said but felt an overwhelming dread.

The queen stood up and smiled down at him. "Thank you my son." She gave him a hug and left the large cooking room.

Tre sat at the table, unsure of what to do or where to go. He decided to go see Rin; she could always comfort him when he was troubled. A ride to Rinland would get him out of the castle. He had not seen Rin since she had a land named for her. Knowing Rin as he did, he was sure she would be embarrassed but proud at the honor, and he wanted to congratulate her.

Since his accident Tre had forgotten Skylin's warning about the old woman and the birds. Skylin was adamant something was wrong and that the birds were messengers. He knew she was right. Her uncanny connection with animals was now beginning to make sense. Ancient farland being ruled by magic, Mallrok descending from the guard line, and the legend about the twin warriors made shivers run down his back when he thought about them.

* * *

Tre was surprised when he saw the new village; he had been lost in thought, leaving the large horse to find his way. When Pat stopped in front of the bakery, Moon hurried out to meet them. Moon loved the big red horse and always brought him a treat. "Are you okay?" she asked as she patted the white patch on the horse's head.

"I'm fine thanks to Old Nanny. She is a great healer," Tre answered.

"Good. We were worried when Skylin told us. Is she coming?" Moon asked.

"No, I came on my own. I can't stay long but wanted to see Mother, I mean Rin." At times Tre was unsure how to refer to the woman who had rescued and raised him.

"She's in the back," Moon told him.

As Tre entered the bakery he fondly remembered the smell of baking bread and the happy memories it brought to mind. The large bakery was filled with tables to feed the villagers while their homes were built. The cooking and sharing of meals was a more efficient way to manage the food supplies, so the villagers agreed to continue doing it until their first harvest. Wiping her hands on her apron, Rin hurried from the back. "Tre we have been so worried. Let me look at your leg." Rin lifted the cloth bandage and was shocked at how it had healed. "It's amazing," she exclaimed. "There are hardly any scars."

"Old Nanny knows a lot about healing plants," Tre explained.

Rin put her arm around Tre and said, "Come have something to eat." Rin and Moon always wanted to feed him, and today Tre was grateful since breakfast was hours past. He was at the table eating a stew of venison and vegetables when Axe and Dellis entered the bakery.

"Tre, we're glad you're here. You need to talk to Rin. She'll listen to you," Dellis said. Tre could tell his friends were upset and motioned for them to join him at the table. Axe pulled out a long wooden bench, and he and Dellis sat down across from Tre. Axe grunted and made a motion with his hands, looking to Dellis to interpret. Dellis nodded to Axe and then looked across at Tre. He began, "It's the old woman who showed up a few weeks ago. Something isn't right. We have been watching her. She is sneaking around, and those boys who came with her will disappear and then suddenly show up."

Tre told his friends, "Skylin said the same thing."

"That's not the weird part. She has started making bundles from sticks. She selects certain ones, ties them together, and mumbles words, then sets them on the ground. Those big blackbirds hanging around will swoop down and fly off with them. Something isn't right," Dellis said again. Axe pounded the table with his large fist, adding his agreement and causing Tre's bowl to bounce.

"Could she be sending messages to someone?" Tre wondered out loud, thinking about Skylin's warning of the birds being messengers.

Axe grunted loudly and clapped his hands to show he agreed with Tre. Dellis looked shocked at the idea, "I—I don't know," he stuttered.

Rin and Moon walked over, hearing the last part of the conversation. "Who is sending messages?" Rin asked.

Tre turned to face his mother. Honesty was important between them. "It's the old woman. Dellis and Axe have been watching her, and something is not right. Even Skylin is worried about her and those birds."

"She is a harmless old woman just trying to keep from starving," Rin objected and placed her hands on her hips. "How could she be sending messages?" she demanded to know.

Knowing it would be hard to win an argument with Rin without proof, Tre tried to explain. "Dellis and Axe have been watching her sort different sizes of sticks, and then she ties them up in bundles and chants words. When she sets them on the ground the birds fly off with them." There, it was all out in the open. Tre quickly added, "And Skylin said those big blackbirds are messengers." He knew Rin trusted Skylin as much as he did.

"Different sizes of sticks?" Rin's brow wrinkled as she thought. She bit her lip and looked at Moon's long brown braids tied with bands of colorful beads and feathers. The old woman had made the colorful ties and insisted on braiding Moon's hair with them. Rin moved beside Moon and lifted one of the braids, looking at it with a strange expression on her face. She quickly began untying the braids, allowing Moon's hair to cascade down her back. Rin carried the bundle of colorful ties and threw them into the fire in the baking hearth.

A strange thing happened when the ties caught fire: they started sparking and crackling, and soon all the colors of the rainbow glowed brightly from the fire. Rin was the only one who didn't look amazed, as Tre, Dellis, Axe, and Moon stood with mouths open, watching the fireplace glow and sparkle.

"What is going on?" Moon's voice was shaky.

Rin turned and faced the bewildered group. "I had forgotten," Rin said, "the lowlanders would use sticks of various shapes to send messages. The different sizes mean certain things."

She looked at Moon and explained, "Before a young girl was given to a warrior, the women would decorate her braids. It was a ritual to burn the braids on their wedding night. How could I have been so stupid!" Rin's face turned red with anger. She looked at Dellis and shouted, "Bring the old woman to me!"

Chapter 14

Following Rin's orders, Dellis and Axe ran from the bakery. Moon slumped down on the wooden bench beside Tre. Her hands started shaking at the mention of the lowlanders, recalling the horrible experience that still caused her to wake up at night, trembling. Tre put his arm around Moon's slim shoulders. "You're safe, Moon. The lowlanders are gone," Tre reassured her. He wished he believed his words.

Moments later, Dellis and Axe rushed into the bakery out of breath. "She's gone," Dellis declared as he gulped for air. "There is no sign of her or the two boys, and all their things are missing. We ran all around the village, and no one saw them leave."

Axe made a sound and moved his arms like wings flapping. "Those birds are gone too," Tre interpreted for Axe.

"Good riddance. She was up to no good. I let the men know to be on the lookout for her and not let her back into Rinland," Dellis stated.

Rinland—Tre remembered the reason for his visit was to tease his mother about having a land name for her, but now was not the time.

Night had crept up, catching Tre by surprise. Dealing with the old woman and all the concerns she caused, he had not been aware of how late it had become. He intended to be back to the castle before dark and did not want to ride Pat at night, the large horse could step in a hole and break a leg. "I need to leave." Tre stood and hugged his mother. "I'll return soon. Do not let that old woman back in the village," he warned Rin as he left the bakery.

Tre was careful to keep Pat at a slow trot on the return trip. When the road turned and started down toward the castle, Tre could smell smoke and could see orange flickers dotting the long valley. He urged Pat into a run, knowing it was dangerous for the horse, but his fear for Fairland was greater. When Pat galloped into the town square, Tre pulled the large horse to a sudden halt and yelled to a man loading a cart with containers of water, "What is going on?"

The man holding the reins of the cart horse yelled back, "Fairland is on fire!"

Tre could distinguish the fires more clearly across the valley floor and urged the big red horse to a full gallop through the town and down the path that led to the castle. Tre jumped from Pat's back and ran into the castle. "Mother!" he called out, fear gripping his throat. The empty hall echoed his voice. He continued running until he reached the large banquet room, where he saw Queen Laurel looking out of a large window at the fires in the valley below. She turned when Tre rushed into the room.

"What is happening?" Tre asked in panic.

"Somehow the slags drugged the men guarding the storage barns and set the barns on fire with the torches meant to keep them away. Mallrok has organized the townspeople to bring water for the fires, but I feel it will be too late." The queen sounded exhausted.

"What purpose will be gained from burning the barns?" Tre was confused—with all the food gone, everyone would starve.

"I don't know." The queen shook her head, looking defeated from this latest turn of events.

"What can I do?" Tre asked, feeling like he let the queen down by returning to the castle after dark.

"Wait with me for Mallrok to report back. He may need you," the queen replied.

"Where is Skylin?" Tre was worried; he had not seen his sister all day.

"She is with Mallrok. She was the one who raised the alarm when she saw the fires start. Thanks to her quick action, we may be able to save some of last year's harvest," the queen explained.

Tre understood what Skylin had been doing all day: watching for the raiders from the high mountain trails. Old Nanny shuffled into the room carrying a tray with steaming bowls of broth and a loaf of freshly baked bread. She set the tray down on a nearby table and said, "Come and eat my queen. You will need your strength to get through this night."

The queen replied, "Thank you Veerna."

Tre and Queen Laurel had finished eating when Mallrok and Skylin came into the room, their clothes torn and covered in soot from the fires. Queen Laurel hurried over to meet them and anxiously asked, "How bad is the damage?"

Mallrok answered, "We won't know how much grain we lost until morning reports. We managed to save most of the barns, but two burnt so fast we couldn't save them. The slags didn't set fire to all the barns."

"How were the guards overtaken?" Tre was curious to know.

"Blow darts dipped in poison made the men pass out. I heard one of the men say a long time ago darts like these were used to hunt animals. The slags snuck up in the dark and shot the guards. We found darts outside all the barns." Mallrok paused and looked at the queen. "It will be a long night, Queen Laurel, and you should get some rest. We won't have a final count of the losses until daylight." Mallrok was always concerned for the queen.

"I'm fine. Besides, I couldn't sleep," the queen replied as she sat back down at the table.

Throughout the long night men arrived at the castle to give updates on the damage to each barn. From their reports, Mallrok figured they had lost one-half of the stored grains. Early in the morning a man from the far valley barns rushed in to report that the far barns had been raided and the grain was carried off in the night. The guards had been knocked out with the poisoned darts, and the slags had emptied the barns. The man bent over, exhausted from his long run.

Mallrok hit the table with his fist and exclaimed, "Now I understand the burning of the barns. While everyone was battling the fires, it gave the slags time to empty the barns at the far end of the valley. What a devious plan by Haaman." Mallrok scowled as he shook his head. Even with all his planning Haaman had outsmarted him.

Skylin jumped up with her fists clenched and her eyes flashing in anger. "We must get the harvest back! The slags cannot be allowed to get away with this." She turned to Mallrok and exclaimed, "Fairland must fight."

Mallrok did not respond to Skylin's outburst but looked at Queen Laurel, who gave a slight nod of her head that the twins did not see.

The queen moved to Skylin's side and said, "Come, we must get you cleaned up. Mallrok is tired and needs to rest." Mallrok stood and bowed, then left the room. Tre was confused. Was Queen Laurel going to let the slags get away with the destruction to the barns they caused and food they stole?

Left alone in the room, Tre didn't know what to do. Daylight was brightening the windows, but he wasn't tired, despite staying awake all night. He was too agitated to sleep. He decided to go and help rebuild the barns. Tre worked hard all day alongside the men, doing any task that was asked of him. It was after dark when he returned to the castle, and he was so exhausted that he fell into bed in his dirty clothes.

"Get up," Skylin ordered as she threw open the door to Tre's room. She quickly pulled back the heavy curtains that covered the window. Tre moaned as the bright midday light burned through his eyelids. Skylin grabbed his leather riding outfit from his wardrobe and tossed it on the bed. "Get dressed!" she said and then quickly added, "We have to catch Mallrok and the army."

Tre sat up in bed and tried to open his eyes. He had worked hard yesterday rebuilding the barns and was still exhausted. His back was sore, and the blisters on his hands hurt. "What are you talking about?" he mumbled.

"Mallrok and the army left at first light to reach the slags before nightfall. They want to be in place and ready when those horrible creatures creep out of their caves." Skylin's startling announcement woke Tre.

Now wide awake, he asked, "Why weren't we told?"

"Mother probably didn't want us in another battle. The guard outside thought I knew and told me of the plan. Get dressed. I'll wait for you out front." There was no curbing Skylin's enthusiasm.

"There is no way we can catch the army in time," Tre reasoned. The sun was already high in the sky. "What about something to eat?" He hadn't eaten in over a day, and last night he was too tired to think of food.

Skylin turned at the door; her eyes alight with anticipation. "There is no time for food. We might miss the battle!" She turned and ran from the room, her footsteps echoing away.

Tre slowly climbed out of bed and dressed in his leather outfit that matched his twin. He picked up his old knife from the table by the window. It was as sharp as the day the butcher gave it to him. The knife gave him a sense of comfort as he secured it in his wide leather belt. After tying his boots, he started downstairs to join his twin, not feeling Skylin's enthusiasm for the coming fight.

From the hallway he could see Skylin astride Wind. The trim gray stallion was stomping the ground anxiously, sensing her excitement. Pat, Tre's large red horse, stood quietly as he waited for his rider. Tre grabbed hold of Pat's long red mane and jumped on his wide back. Skylin tossed Tre his large staff and told him, "You will need this, brother. Those slags are sneaky creatures. Let's go!" she yelled and kicked Wind in the side. The swift gray horse took off like the wind.

Tre felt uncertain about the fight ahead and looked up at the large castle, thinking could this be his last battle. From an upstairs window, Queen Laurel stood watching as her children rode to battle, a battle she had wanted them to avoid. Tre lifted his staff to his mother, and she returned his salute with a wave of her hand. "Let's go, Pat," Tre said, kicking the side of the large red horse, who galloped down the path to town, following Skylin.

The big horse quickly caught up to Skylin. Seeing the twins riding down the path to town, the townspeople stepped onto the cobblestone road and formed a column for the twins to ride between. Everyone lifted one arm high, with fist closed in the Fairland battle salute, knowing where the twins were heading and wishing them victory. Side by side, they rode—The Twins of Fairland.

Chapter 15

The twins rode between the guard line formed by the town people and entered the long valley. When the horses reached full stride, Tre held tight to Pat's long red mane, knowing if he fell off at this speed he would break his neck. Skylin rode with ease on the back of Wind, at one with her gray stallion. A large yellow blur raced down from the mountain and ran alongside Wind. It was Cerra. The big cat easily matched the pace of the horses. Wind gave a whinny, acknowledging the cat. It shocked Tre that Wind and Cerra knew each other and had traveled together before. There were many things he still didn't know about his sister.

A large shadow blocked the midday sun, and Tre glanced up, wondering where the clouds came from; it was clear and sunny when they rode from town. He grinned. It was no cloud, but one very large owl that had joined them. Koda flew with ease, his large wings carrying him high above them. Koda gave a loud screech and flew on ahead, scouting for any unseen perils that may await them. Tre felt more confident about the battle ahead now that Koda and Cerra had joined them.

*   *   *

Mallrok and the army reached the end of the valley just before the sun started to fade. Mallrok's strategy was to deploy the men among the rocks at the mountain base. There the army would hide and surprise the slags when they left their caves to raid the valley. Besides bows and arrows, the men carried torches. They did not want to battle the slags in the dark. It would be too easy for the slags to sneak up and shoot poison darts. They had not stopped for food since leaving early that morning, and water and rations were passed around to the exhausted men.

As dusk engulfed the valley, noises could be heard from inside the mountain, and scraping sounds became louder. From their hiding place, the army men could make out shapes emerging from the hidden caves. A lone figure clothed in a robe of brown fabric emerged and stood on a ledge. As he stood upright, he leaned on a large carved stick of wood for balance. He motioned for the skinny white creatures to gather around.

Before the robed figure could give orders for the night's raid, Mallrok stepped out from behind a large boulder and called out, "Haaman, what is this, more of your sneaky tricks?" Startled by Mallrok's appearance, the creatures scurried back into the mountain.

Haaman, the slags' mystic leader, twisted around to face Mallrok, using the large stick for balance. He could have been a younger version of Mallrok. "Mallrok, you are either very brave or very stupid to come here." Haaman sneered.

The two mystics faced each other, one clothed in a white robe and one in a brown robe. The slags began to creep out, and, seeing their leader was not afraid of the white-robed stranger, they became bolder. In the dark huge animal eyes began to appear behind the slags, glowing eerily. The slags and the animals' numbers increased as they emerged from the mountain.

"I have come to demand that you stop the raids. You cannot steal from Fairland any longer." Mallrok's loud voice was firm.

"We are only taking what was promised by Kross," Haman shouted back.

"Kross is dead and was never king of Fairland." Mallrok was not backing down in the face of increasing peril emerging from the mountain.

"We kept our end of the treaty and have the right to take what was promised!" With his stick, Haaman struck the ledge, and sparks flew around him.

"That agreement is over," Mallrok yelled back and held his staff tight.

"Who will stop us? You are old and weak," Haaman scorned.

To demonstrate his power, Haaman made a circle with one arm, and a large ball of light formed in his hand. He threw the glowing orb at Mallrok's feet, where it hit and sizzled and burned. "The next one will strike you, and you will burn like your barns." The anger on Haaman's face glowed in the light from the fire ball. At the threat to Mallrok, Blane and the army men stepped from their hiding places with weapons drawn and torches now lit.

The appearance of the armed men with blazing torches caused the large eyed animals to hiss loudly, baring sharp teeth as they backed away from the light. The slags shielded their eyes with their long boney arms. "Your torches will burn out, and then you will be part of our world," Haaman warned and then challenged Mallrok. "Let's end this now."

Haaman's warning was true. Once the torches burned down the slags would attack with their poison darts and long, sharp claws. Mallrok knew he could not match the magic powers of Haaman. "Time is on our side," Haaman laughed loudly as one by one the small torches the men held begin to flicker.

Haaman raised his arm to signal the slags to attack, when a loud screech echoed overhead. Mallrok looked up and saw Koda, his huge wings causing a whirlwind. Haaman startled at the sight of the large bird and lowered his arm. Koda flew down and perched in a tree, looking menacingly at Haaman.

Suddenly Cerra sprang from the dark, landing beside Mallrok. The big cat sensed the badgerlike animals hiding in the dark and loudly growled. It was a warning the lurking animals understood; if they came any closer they would face Cerra's wrath. Haaman began shaking his head from side to side, unsure what to do about the large bird and big cat.

Side by side, Wind and Pat crashed into the opening behind the boulders where the army waited. The horses slid to a stop, causing dust to swirl around, their breath like smoke coming from their flared nostrils. Skylin and Tre jumped from their mounts and ran to Mallrok, ready to defend him at any cost.

Haaman was astounded at the sudden arrival of the twins, and he looked hard at their staffs, exact replicas of Mallrok's. "Who are these two, and why are they here?" Haaman shrieked.

Mallrok pointed to the twins standing at his side and announced, "The Twins of Fairland, as foretold by the old ones."

Haaman glared at the twins and wildly shook his head. He moved around in a circle on the ledge. "No!" he screamed and threw down his stick. Using both hands in a twisting motion, he formed a large crackling ball of fire. He pulled his arm back and threw it straight at Mallrok.

Instantly, the twins stepped in front of Mallrok and crossed their staffs to protect him from the flaming ball. When the staffs crossed, Skylin's bumped Tre's, and a bolt of lightning spewed from the top of both. The ball of fire Haaman threw at Mallrok hit the staffs where they crossed and disintegrated. Its menacing magic could not withstand the power of the twins' staffs.

Skylin laughed out loud, delighted with her staff's new power. She pointed it at Haaman, and a bolt of lightning sparked the rock beside him. "The next one will be aimed at your head," she yelled at the stunned mystic. Startled by the lightning bolt, the slags crawled back toward their caves, their boldness dissolving.

Haaman suddenly disappeared from the ledge, but his high-pitched screams could be heard issuing orders for the slags to attack.

Mallrok quickly turned to Blane, "Get the men to cover," he yelled as the torches started to flicker out. Darkness would soon engulf them. Cerra growled and sensed the badgerlike animals that dwelled in the mountain coming closer. Skylin and Tre hurried Mallrok to the protection of the boulders.

Whizzing noises filled the air as the slags started to attack with their poisoned darts. One of the army men screamed out that he was hit, and others held him as he slid down the side of the boulder, unconscious. Then another yelled out that he was also hit. "We have to do something. We are easy targets in the dark," Skylin yelled at Tre. When Tre didn't respond she demanded, "You're the smart one—think of something."

In the darkness the staffs bumped, and a flicker of light appeared. "Stand up," Tre ordered.

"Are you crazy? We'll be hit for sure," Skylin scoffed.

Tre grabbed her arm. "Stand up and cross the staffs." She immediately understood his plan.

"Great idea, brother," she said as she stood up. Together the twins stepped into the open area and crossed their staffs. A bright light spewed from the top of each staff and lit up the area brighter than day.

The slags were blinded by the sudden brightness, and they staggered around. Blane led the army from behind the boulders. The slags were easy targets for the Fairland archers, and flying arrows began to hit the blinded creatures. Screaming from injured slags filled the air. The army quickly surrounded them, stopping their retreat back into the mountain.

The slags were now circled by the Fairland army, cowering down, shielding their eyes from the bright light. Mallrok stepped forward and yelled, "Haaman, show yourself!" The mystic walked out from behind the ledge and fell to his knees, trembling in front of Mallrok, his balance stick rolling to one side. Haaman had never seen anything like the power of the twin's staffs, nor animals the size of Cerra and Koda.

"We should finish them now," Skylin roared as she pointed her staff, ready to burn each and every skinny creature to a crisp by lightning bolts.

"Stop," Tre told his twin as he stepped forward. He looked at the cowering Haaman. "For years there has been peace between our clans. Can it not be that way again?"

Haaman looked up, startled at the turn of events, sure that he was going to be killed. He was confused and asked, "Who are you?"

Mallrok stepped to Tre's side and said, "The rightful king of Fairland."

Tre leaned down and picked up the stick Haaman had been holding, examining it closely. The end was covered in the same metal as the old knife he carried. "Do you get this metal from the mountains?" Tre asked the cowering leader.

"Yes. We dig it out and other things. It is what we traded Kross for food," Haaman admitted. Skylin stood watching Haaman, on guard, ready to use her staff if he tried to harm her twin.

Tre turned to Mallrok and said, "I've read about using metal to make tools to work the ground. These tools will make it easier and faster to plant and harvest, and we can expand the crops."

Mallrok looked at the metal-covered stick Tre held and realized aloud, "This is why Kross was able to arm his men so fast. Metal used for weapons can also be used for tools." Mallrok nodded in agreement at Tre's suggestion.

Tre faced Haaman, "Do you speak for your people?" he asked the cowering mystic.

"Yes." Haaman was hesitant and unsure before the young king.

"I will make a new treaty with you. Fairland will trade the metal you dig from the mountain for grain and cattle. But not until this year's harvest is gathered will the slags receive any more grain. Fairland barely has enough grain left for food and planting crops. There can be no more raids." Skylin was amazed at her brother's boldness. He stood as regal as Mallrok as he faced the devious slag leader.

Haaman knew he could agree to the new treaty or face the destruction of the slag clan. "I will agree to the new treaty," Haaman said as he looked up at the young king. He saw honesty in Tre's face and knew he could trust the king's word.

"Both clans will benefit from this treaty, and we can once again dwell in peace." Tre reached out a hand to the mystic leader of the slags. Haaman slowly stood up and clasped Tre's hand, sealing the new treaty between the two clans.

"Tell your people to bring out as much of this metal as they can. We will begin making the tools needed to plant and harvest." Tre felt relief the slag leader had agreed with the new treaty and there would be no more raids.

Haaman bowed and turned to face the slags and, leaning on his stick for support, gave new orders. The army men moved aside to allow the slags to carry their wounded back into the mountain.

Skylin felt her knife secured in her belt. She liked her weapons, but her brother was right. To continue to fight the slags would eventually lead to the destruction of Fairland.

Mallrok placed his arm around Tre's shoulders and said, "I'm proud at the way you handled this situation. You are wise beyond your years."

Skylin was listening and added, "It's all those books he reads." She laughed out loud in her annoying way.

Tre looked up and saw Koda perched above. "Koda, go back to the castle and let the queen know everything is okay." Koda flapped his large wings and flew off toward the castle.

Tre turned to Mallrok. "We have a lot of work ahead of us. We need to arrange for wagons to haul the metal back to town and let the blacksmith know he is going to be busy." Tre yawned. "Right now I think I'll share some rations with the men and get some sleep."

"Always thinking of yourself," Skylin teased her brother.

The Twins of Fairland

Part 4

The Forgotten

Chapter 16

The Fairland people finished gathering the harvest, and it was the largest in Fairland's history. Everyone in the kingdom was thankful the monthly rations were over. The new metal tools made working the fields much easier and faster for the crop tenders, and the new tools did not constantly break like the old wood ones did. Haaman kept his bargain, and the slags delivered enough metal to make tools for Fairland and Rinland, keeping the town's blacksmith very busy. Under the leadership of Queen Laurel and Tre, it had been a year of challenge and change for the people of Fairland: working with the slags, learning new ways to grow crops, teaching the Rinland villagers how to raise crops and cattle.

Instructed by the Fairland crop tenders, the Rinland village men quickly learned how to plow fields and plant crops. Axe led the men to get the large meadow ready to plant, and he worked from first light until last light to make sure the crops were planted on schedule. Rin teased him, saying he was like an expectant father, daily watering the new seedlings and watching them grow. As the crops grew, so did the villagers' excitement, knowing they would have enough food for the coming year and would not have to depend on Fairland for help. After all the crops were harvested, the villagers celebrated in the bakery with a special meal prepared by Rin and Moon.

During the past year a friendship had developed between Mallrok and Haaman. Mallrok would accompany the weekly cart to pick up the metal from the slags and spend the night hours talking with Haaman of the old times. Mallrok learned that deep inside the mountain, the slags had kept record of their history, and their language was a variation of that in the old records in the castle library. Tre always waited for Mallrok to return from the trip and learn more of Fairland's history.

Tre spent the morning with Queen Laurel going over the harvest reports. All the barns were full, and the two barns that had burnt during the slags raid had been rebuilt, larger and more efficient. Inside the new barns, Tre instructed the wood workers to build rows of shelving with large bins. This made it easier to separate the crops and plan for the coming winter. The barns closest to the mountain edge were filled and set aside for the slags. Mallrok and Haaman had agreed on the amount of grain and livestock to exchange for the metal the slags mined from the mountains. The new treaty with the slags was working well, and they were no longer enemies but partners. The people of Fairland had been willing to work the long hours needed to rebuild the barns and get the fields ready for planting, knowing the results of their hard labor would benefit them, not be used for the king's personal wealth like when Kross ruled. Queen Laurel led Fairland by a council made up of representatives from the town and crop tenders. This openness allowed everyone to understand the issues and give input to their council member.

After the last report was reviewed, Tre left the room so his mother could meet with the council. He was hungry and on his way to see what Old Nanny was cooking when Skylin ran up behind him. She looked excited and Tre wondered if she ever slowed down. "Where have you been this morning?" he asked as they entered the large cooking room.

Skylin took a gulp of air. "I've been at the Celebration of Harvest meeting. We are going to have more games this year than ever, and I intend to enter every one." Her face glowed with anticipation.

Tre told her, "I'm sure all the young men can't wait to have you beat them again this year."

Skylin hurried past him, ignoring his comment. "I need to get something to eat. Then I'm riding to Rinland to tell them about the festival. Everyone at the meeting agreed to invite them, and they can enter the games too." She pulled open the door to the large pantry where old nanny stored food and filled her arms with bread, churned butter, and slices of meat. The pantry had been carved deep inside the mountain and was always cold inside. "Do you want to come with me?" she asked her brother while she filled her mouth with food.

A ride to Rinland seemed like a good idea to Tre. He had been very busy the past year, working with the metal crafter to design the new tools for farming, meeting with the crop tenders to determine the best tool for each crop, and then overseeing the building and modifying of the barns. He had not seen Rin in months. "Sounds like a good idea. Pass me the bread," he agreed and joined his twin at the table.

It was a good feeling to be riding Pat alongside Skylin and Wind. Tre missed the long rides to the end of the valley and back, riding fast like the wind and Skylin never wanting to slow down. Skylin broke the silence and asked, "Are you going to enter the games?"

"No," Tre answered. He had no interest in participating in knife-throwing, archery, battling with swords for points, or riding and throwing lances into straw; they brought back painful memories. He would get no enjoyment from the games.

"You're just afraid I'll beat you," Skylin boasted.

"I know you will beat me," Tre admitted.

Tre looked over at his twin, knowing the ride to Rinland was really her excuse to personally invite Dellis. Her deviousness didn't fool him. "Will you beat Dellis in the games or let him win?" Tre teased her. Skylin glared back at Tre and then nudged Wind into a run, leaving Tre and Pat in her dust. Tre decided he had enough of her attitude and nudged Pat in the sides, "Let's show her who is the fastest," he said, and, at his urging, the large horse lengthened his stride to a full gallop and quickly gained on Wind. Before the racing twins entered the long meadow, Pat was far ahead. Tre slowed the big red horse, not wanting to tear up the plowed land with the horse's hooves, and waited for his sister to catch up.

"You've been holding back, brother. I never knew Patch could outrun Wind." Tre had worried that Skylin would be upset about losing the race to him, but it was surprise at the large horse's speed that showed on her face. A fair battle and the outcome always settled the matter for Skylin. "No one could beat Patch in the races," she told him.

"That's why I'm not entering. Let someone else win," Tre answered. Skylin looked confused. "You don't always have to win," he tried to explain to his sister.

"Would you race against Dellis if it wasn't a fair race?" Tre purposely brought his best friend into the conversation.

He knew Dellis was becoming fond of his sister and wondered how she felt. Skylin halted Wind and jumped off his back. Tre did the same with Pat, and together they walked toward the village, leading their horses.

Finally she answered, "No. He is the only one who has treated me like a person. Everyone in Fairland shunned me like an outcast. After you came back things changed, but I still remember how it felt." This was the first time Skylin talked about her feelings, and Tre was surprised, having thought nothing bothered his twin. Her friendship with Dellis was built on openness and trust, and Tre was pleased that Skylin realized the good qualities in friend.

Tre stopped and looked around. He was proud that the new village had been named for his mother. Rin had rescued him and determinedly raised him as her son. The bond he shared with her stayed strong. The buildings were completed and the small village was thriving. There was a new leather shop where you could trade for vests, belts, or moccasins. "Come on," Skylin urged Tre forward. She was anxious to reach the bakery. It was time for the evening meal, and everyone would be there.

When they reached the bakery, smells of baked bread drifted in the air. Skylin dropped Wind's reins and hurried inside. Tre tied both horses to the post and noticed a new grain shed. It was hastily built but would last the year, and plans were being made to build a barn next year like the new ones in Fairland. There had been a lot of changes in the past year for the villagers. They moved to the large meadow, rebuilt their burnt homes, learned to plant and grow crops, and now had a small herd of cattle and pens of pigs and chickens.

As Tre stepped into the bakery he could hear Skylin inviting everyone to the Celebration of Harvest festival. Rin and Moon were busy dishing out food, so Tre sat down at a back table. He could talk to Rin while they ate. She and Moon did the cooking, and the other women handled the clearing and washing of dishes. He was glad Rin now had adequate help with the chore of feeding everyone. The butcher delivered fresh meat daily, and Axe kept her supplied with vegetables and grain. The butcher's wife carried a plate of food over to Tre. "It's good to see you, Tre. It's been too long," her friendly welcome warmed him.

As he was enjoying the meal, Axe and Dellis entered the bakery. "Tre, it's about time you visited." Dellis rushed over and slapped Tre on the back.

Tre stood up and grabbed hold of his friend's shoulders. "It's great to see you too." Axe came up and heartedly shook Tre's hand with a wide smile on his face.

The two men joined Tre at the table, and while they ate Dellis told Tre of all the improvements that had been made. "It's amazing at all the progress we made during the past year after we arrived hurt, bandaged, and empty handed. I wish the ones we lost could see Rinland." Dellis had a faraway look, and Tre knew he was thinking of Windel, their small friend who had died while defending the high mountain village.

Skylin came over, sat down across from Tre, and told him, "Rin said everyone will come to the celebration, and she will let them know about the games if they want to participate." Skylin looked at Dellis and explained, "Every year after the harvest, Fairland holds a celebration with games and food. You should make sure Cary enters the archery competition."

Dellis looked across the table at Skylin and said, "I'll make sure he does. Will you be entering the games?"

She grinned across the table at him and admitted, "Most of them."

Dellis laughed, "Yeah all the ones you can win."

*   *   *

When the twins returned from Rinland, Tre went to the library and picked up the worn leather-covered book he was trying to read. It was written in the old scribe, and he was sure a word translated into serpent, but it could mean snake or maybe viper. It was another riddle he was trying to solve. The ink had faded from age, and he moved the book closer to the candle to try to make out words that were no longer visible.

"Careful or your nose will get stuck on the page." Skylin laughed at her own joke and then told him, "You look like some old man bent over like that."

Tre sat back in his chair and looked up at his sister. "It's another old myth, but the words have worn off, and I can't read the last line," he explained to her.

"I can't understand why you spend all your time with your nose stuck in books." She shook her head, not understanding his fascination with the old myths.

"It's our history, and the last one proved to be true," Tre pointed out.

"The twins of the guard line," she recalled, her eyes alight, reliving the battle with the slags and the power of her staff.

"Listen to what I've completed," Tre said, and Skylin flopped down next to him, trying not to show her interest. Slowly Tre read the ancient script.

> *The Serpent will come to kill and to claim*
> *Farland as his domain*
> *Leader against Leader must fight to the end*
> *Good over Evil can only win*
> *If the power of the staff conquers the serpent's wrath*
> *Cast down . . .*

"I can't make out any words after 'cast down.'" Tre pointed to where the words faded away into the page.

Skylin looked at Tre and shrugged. "Well if it's a snake, cut its head off. That's how to kill a snake."

"It's not always that simple with these old legends. 'The serpent' could mean something or someone and not an actual snake," Tre tried to explain.

"Well those old guys who scribbled this down should have said what they meant," Skylin huffed as she stood up. "It's late, and I'm going to bed. I need to be up early; I only have two days to practice for the games." Tre watched his sister walk from the room, and then he carefully closed the old book. He didn't share her attitude toward the old legends. He felt they had been written down for a purpose. He held the book close and rubbed his hand over the worn cover. He sensed the myth was a warning, but without the final words it was useless.

* * *

At the Celebration of Harvest festival, Skylin held true to her word. She entered each of the games, but lost to Cary in the archery competition. Wind won the horse race, coming in far ahead of the other horses. It had been a day of celebration, with games, feasting, and dancing all night. Rin and the villagers were welcomed, and many new friendships were made that day. Tre introduced Rin to Old Nanny, who agreed to share her healing poultice and show Rin where to find the special plants. Queen Laurel's opening speech acknowledged everyone for their hard work the past year and their willingness to help the villagers rebuild their lives. From all the cheering and shouting after her speech, it was evident how much the queen was loved.

Tre enjoyed watching everyone have fun, and it gave him more pleasure than winning any game ever could. Under Old Nanny's supervision there was ample food, and the wild berry cobbler had everyone going back for seconds, thirds for Skylin and Axe. Rin pulled Tre onto the dance floor, and they danced one of the mountain jigs she had taught him. Then she grabbed Moon to dance with Tre while she and Axe danced the next jig. The wooden floor shook with each hop that Axe made in time to the music causing the other dancers to bend over with laughter. The full moon was starting to go down when the last of the revelers left for home. It would take all the next day to clean up the town square, but Tre was sure no one would complain. It had been a great Celebration of Harvest.

Chapter 17

Rin was in the back of the bakery when the door slammed open. Startled by the noise, she looked out and saw Axe bent over and breathless from running. She hurried out and asked, "Axe what is wrong?" She had never seen him this upset. He motioned for her to get Dellis; his sign for Dellis was to grab his right wrist. Rin nodded she understood and told him to sit down. Axe shook his head and moved about, too agitated to sit. Rin found Dellis in the leather shop and told him something had upset Axe. As he hurried with Rin to the bakery, Dellis told her, "He left to go hunting this morning. I wonder what happened."

When Rin and Dellis entered the bakery, Axe was pacing back and forth. Rin took his large hands in hers and led him to a table. "Sit down and let me get you some water. Then you can tell us what is wrong." She quickly filled a mug with water from a wooden bucket, brought it to him, and sat down beside him, placing her hand on his arm to calm him. Dellis sat across the table wondering what had upset his large friend. When Axe finished quenching his thirst, he began to motion with his hands. Dellis watched closely and interpreted, "You left to go hunting and came to the tree bridge and went across it to hunt." Axe nodded. Then he pointed two fingers at his eyes, stood up, and walked to the door of the bakery. He pointed outside to the ground in front of the bakery, held up three fingers, and looked at Dellis. "You saw in the mountains, three what?" Dellis pondered.

Axe walked outside, and Dellis followed him. Axe pointed to the ground and held up one finger and raised his hand to shoulder height and then two fingers and held his hand half way to the ground. He looked at Dellis, held out three fingers, and then he made like his long arms were wings and flapped them. "You saw the old woman and two boys across the river," Dellis said and gasped when he understood what Axe was miming. Axe cupped his hands and wiggled his fingers. "They are camping and have a fire." Axe looked relieved and clapped his hands to signal Dellis had it correct. "Did you see those blackbirds too?" Dellis asked. Axe shook his head for no. Dellis looked worried and went back inside to tell Rin.

When Rin heard that the old woman had returned, she insisted that Dellis and Axe go find her and make her leave. Rin thought for a moment and then called after them, "Wait, I'm coming with you. I can understand her." Rin took off her apron and went to let Moon know she would be away for a while but did not tell her the reason. Moon could handle the food preparation for the evening meal and was becoming as good a cook as Rin. "Be careful," Moon called after Rin as she left the bakery.

Rin caught up with Dellis and Axe where the tree spanned the deep river gorge. They had run most of the way and stopped to catch their breath before crossing the slippery bridge. Dellis whispered to Axe, "Where did you see them?" Axe pointed to Rin and then formed a tent with his hands. "Near the old hut where Rin lived?" Dellis asked, and Axe nodded. Dellis said, "I'll go across first. Then Rin, and Axe will cross last. Only one of us at a time on the bridge." Slowly the three crept to the fallen tree and looked across to the other side. Dellis motioned that he didn't see anything moving and quickly stepped onto the bridge. When he was on the other side, he motioned for Rin to cross and then Axe.

As they start down the mountainside to the small meadow where Rin had lived with Tre, they could smell smoke. When they reached the edge of tree line they saw the collapsed hut was being used for firewood. The old woman and the two boys were sitting around a campfire. Rin stepped out of the tree line and headed directly at the old woman. Startled at seeing Rin quickly coming toward her, the old woman stood up. With her fists clenched in anger, Rin shouted at the old woman in the language she understood, "You leave this place now!"

The two boys jumped up and scurried behind the old woman. Across the campfire, the old woman faced Rin and from black beady eyes glared at her. The old woman reached out and pointed a gnarled finger at Rin and threatened, "The Rider of Upland is coming, and you will be punished for killing Tulac's tribe." Stunned Rin stopped her charge and stared in shock at the old woman, not believing what she just heard. The old woman shook her bent finger at Rin and snarled, "The Rider is coming."

The old woman began chanting words Rin did not understand and then threw a handful of what looked like small stones into the campfire. The campfire exploded with flames leaping so high that it made Rin jump backward to avoid being burnt. Axe and Dellis rushed to Rin's side, unsure of what was happening. When the fire collapsed back to normal, the old woman and two boys had vanished. Dellis ran to the campfire and looked around. There was nowhere for them to hide, but somehow they had disappeared. Axe ran forward with his hands raised in question. "They're gone, but where?" Dellis stammered, at a loss to understand what had happened. Rin quickly started putting the fire out by smothering it with dirt. Axe helped her, and they waited to make sure the fire did not flame back up.

On the way back Dellis said, "I'll place a guard every day at the bridge to watch for them. I still don't understand how they could just disappear."

Rin didn't hear what Dellis said because she was worried about the old woman's reference to Tulac. Had the old woman known all along what happened to the lowlanders and about Rin's part in the rescue? How had the old woman found the villagers in the hidden meadow? Who was The Rider of Upland? She had never heard of such a person or place, and he now was apparently coming to avenge Tulac. Her next worry was how much she should tell Tre and the others.

*   *   *

It had been several days since the Celebration of Harvest, and Tre decided to ride to the meadow to check on Rin. Skylin had left early that morning and didn't tell him where she was going. His sister could have gone ahead to see Dellis, although she would never admit it. From Pat's anxious behavior Tre knew the big horse had been left in the corral too long, but the past months had been extremely busy and left him little time to ride. He had barely settled down on Pat's back before the horse took off down the path that led to the road out of Fairland, his strong legs and large hooves eating up the distance. Tre held tight to Pat's long red mane, knowing it would be useless to try to slow him down. Pat was probably trying to catch up with Wind, and the fast pace would do the horse good.

When Tre rode up to the bakery, he did not see Wind tied up out front. Either his sister had ridden somewhere else or was out riding with Dellis. Tre tied Pat's reins to the post and went inside. The bakery was empty, which was unusual, as it was the local gathering place. Tre walked to the back of the bakery and saw the day's bread cooling next to the stone hearth. He continued out the back door and looked at the far mountains where he had grown up. It seemed so long ago. So much had happened in the past five years since first meeting Skylin. It was getting harder to remember the times spent with Rin in the old hut. Tre looked at the stand of trees beyond the bakery and could see someone. It was Rin, and he wondered why she was standing there. He walked over to where she waited.

"Mother why are you out here?" Tre's question startled Rin, making her jump; she had not heard him approach. From the worried look on her face, Tre could tell something was wrong as he waited for her to answer.

Rin turned back toward the mountains and explained, "I'm waiting for Dellis and Skylin to return. There is something I need to tell you as soon as they get back, but I don't want Moon to hear because it will upset her." Tre wanted to know more, but if Rin was waiting for Dellis to return there must be a reason. In the distance he could see two riders making their way down the mountainside.

"Here they come," Rin said in relief.

Tre asked, "Where is Moon?" If they were keeping something from her, he wanted to make sure she wasn't around to hear.

"She's helping Axe today," Rin replied as Dellis and Skylin rode up.

Rin hurried over and grabbed the reins of Dellis' horse. "Did the guard see anyone?" she anxiously asked him.

"No. Everything is quiet, and he crossed the bridge this morning to make sure," Dellis answered as he slid off the back of the horse.

Skylin was still sitting on Wind and gave Tre a look that spoke of trouble. At times she didn't need words to communicate with him. Slowly she dismounted and walked over to Rin and told her, "You need to tell Tre everything that happened."

Rin sighed and then said, "Let's go back to the bakery."

When they were seated at one of the large wooden tables, Rin told Tre about the old woman coming back and her warning about "The Rider of Upland" coming to avenge Tulac. Rin was concerned and said, "I don't understand how she found us, but all along she knew who we were. I have never heard of The Rider or of Upland, but the old woman was very serious in her threat."

"We were going to run her off, but she threw something into the fire to cause it to flame up. Then she and those two boys just disappeared. We looked for them, but they were gone." Dellis was still uncertain how three people could instantly vanish.

Tre repeated, "The Rider of Upland. I have never read anything about that name. I can ask Mallrok when I get back to the castle. Where is Upland?" He looked at Rin.

She shook her head and shrugged. "I don't know."

"When you were captive, did you ever see the old woman or those birds? You said the lowlanders would communicate with the stick bundles." Tre hated to bring up bad memories for his mother.

Rin bit at her lip as she recalled times she would rather forget. "No I never saw them before. The older boys would run off with the bundles and return in a few days, but I never knew where they went or what any of it meant. Tulac's son was one of the runners, I remember that."

"Did you see what direction they went when they left the camp?" Tre asked.

"Not back across the desert, the way we went, but toward the higher land beyond the campground." Rin looked exhausted, and her shoulders slumped; her worry about the old woman and the threat of The Rider was wearing on her.

Skylin had been quietly listening, but no longer. She glared at Tre and exclaimed, "I told you not to let those lowlanders live. They must have made it to the high land beyond the desert and told this rider what happened to Tulac."

Rin gasped and said, "Tulac's son was part of those allowed to live. He was a runner and knew where to go."

"This just keeps getting better." Skylin scowled as she looked at Tre.

Dellis added, "The guards understand how serious this is and if they see anyone will sound a warning. I'll let the men in the village know to keep their weapons close and be ready."

Tre looked at Rin and asked, "How are you going to keep this from Moon, especially if the village is put on alert." Rin just shook her head, knowing that Moon's bad dreams would get worse once she learned about this new threat.

It was a silent ride back to Fairland with both twins lost in their own thoughts. Tre wasn't sure how he should feel. Had he been wrong to allow the few lowland women and children to live? The threat to Rin and the villagers was again a reality. Maybe the threat could be managed with both sides agreeing to a solution. The problem with the slags had been resolved, and it was working well. As soon as he returned to the castle he would find Mallrok to see if he knew about The Rider and Upland. He knew Skylin was upset with him, but he couldn't change what happened with the desert dwellers, and he didn't know if he could have made a different decision.

When Tre entered the library, Mallrok was waiting for him. Skylin had hurried through feeding and watering Wind, leaving Tre behind. Apparently she had found Mallrok and told him about the new threat. "How serious is it?" Mallrok questioned.

Tre answered, "I'm not sure, but Rin is very upset. Dellis has posted guards at the river bridge to alert the village if they see anyone." Tre sat down by Mallrok and asked, "Have you heard of The Rider or Upland? The old woman, and I think she has mystical powers to vanish like she did, warned Rin that The Rider of Upland is coming to avenge Tulac."

Mallrok scratched his long gray beard in thought, and then he said, "Many generations ago, during the time of the ancient ones, there were others that were jealous of farland and its prosperity and fought to claim our land. They came from beyond the desert and were fierce fighters. Their mystics had dark powers. I don't recall where they came from other than the high land beyond the desert. I do remember they had the ability to change into animals, which gave them an advantage over farland. Farland was losing the battle when the ancients cast the spell that blocked the entrance to the valley. The slags were part of farland and helped fight the dark ones. I'll ask Haaman if he knows more about them or The Rider. Mallrok stood up and left Tre to his worries. Animal changers—could the old woman have that power?

*   *   *

Tre knew Skylin was avoiding him. He hadn't seen her for a few days. She was around the castle because he heard her talking to Old Nanny, and she had been to see their mother because the queen asked Tre about the threat to Rin. Tre looked for any mention of The Rider or Upland in the old books, but he did not find anything. When Mallrok returned from the weekly trip to pick up the mined metal, he had met with Haaman and asked about The Rider and Upland. The writing in the caves only told of a long battle ending with the valley being sealed. Tre had visited Rin yesterday, and the guards had not seen any activity across the bridge. Rin said the village men were on alert, and Moon was staying in the bakery, not venturing outside once she learned of the warning by the old woman.

Tre noticed Skylin walking toward the corral, and he hurried to catch up with her. He was tired of being avoided, and her attitude was not helping either of them. He once longed for her silence, but now he missed talking and sharing things with her. "Skylin, wait up!" he yelled, but she continued walking like she didn't hear him. He caught up with her at the corral. "Look I'm sorry if you're upset with me. There is nothing I can do to change things," he tried to reason with her.

She whirled around and faced him. "I want to hit you I am so mad."

"Go ahead if it will make you feel better. Don't you think I feel bad enough without you making it worse? If something happens to Rin or Moon or anyone in the village, it will be my fault." Tre's face showed his concern. He needed his twin's support and help, not her anger and blame.

Skylin saw Tre's anguished look and said, "I'm sorry. I never thought of how you might feel." She reached out and took his hand. "I shouldn't have acted this way. You wouldn't have," she apologized, which was a rare event.

A sudden swooshing sound caused the twins to look up and see Koda flying toward them. The big owl landed on the corral fence and gave a series of screeching sounds that echoed back and forth between the mountain and the barn. His eyes blazed, and he shifted his large body from foot to foot. "It's a warning," Skylin told her brother. Tre looked away, concerned by what Koda's warning might mean. He didn't notice when Skylin moved next to Koda and whispered low, "Tomorrow."

Tre was worried the old woman had returned and decided he would warn Rin. The next morning, after meeting with his mother and the growers to determine next year's planting and setting aside the correct amount of seed, Tre left the castle and headed for the corral. He told Queen Laurel he was going to go see Rin but omitted to tell her about Koda's warning. Until he knew more, it didn't make sense to cause her worry. Pat was alone in the corral, which meant Skylin had ridden off that morning. He looked around and did not see Koda, but that was not unusual. The owl perched in the tall mountain trees and only came to the castle when needed. Cerra never came into town but watched from the tree line. Everyone had seen the large yellow cat with Skylin but not up close.

Tre dismounted and tied Pat to the post outside the bakery. He didn't see Wind, but Skylin could be out riding with Dellis. He entered the bakery, saw Rin and Dellis sitting at a table, walked over, and sat down. Dellis was telling Rin that there was no sign of the old woman or anyone else around the bridge and the guards were making daily trips across to the other side to make sure.

"That's good news. It won't be long until the winter snow will make it unlikely she will come back. We know how harsh the weather is that high on the mountain." Rin looked tired but managed to smile at Tre. "It's good to see you, son."

Tre hated to bring more bad news but felt he needed to relay Koda's warning. "Have you seen Skylin today? She left early this morning, and I thought she was coming here." Both Rin and Dellis said they had not seen her. Tre sighed and then told them, "Yesterday Koda flew in screeching loud. Skylin said he was bringing us a warning. I thought maybe the old woman had returned."

Rin and Dellis shook their heads, and Dellis said, "No sign of her, and I just returned from the bridge. The guard went across this morning to check. I'm not sure what Koda's warning is about."

Tre told Dellis to keep the guards on alert. He saw Moon standing in the doorway. She looked like she had not been sleeping. Her large brown eyes had dark circles under them. Tre knew she still had bad dreams from being taken captive and feared it happening again. He waved at her as he left the bakery, and she gave a small wave back.

The next day, Queen Laurel found Tre in the library. She walked over and told him, "You know this year will be a special year for you and Skylin." The queen looked excited and her eyes sparkled. "My twins will be officially grown and will celebrate their eighteenth birthday." Actually Tre celebrated two birthdays, one with Rin on the date she had picked out and his actual birthday with Skylin. The queen looked at Tre and said, "I need to think about a betrothal for you and Skylin. You two will be old enough to marry and you can assume the responsibilities of king of Fairland."

Tre was stunned and jumped up, dropping the book he was reading. "What!" he exclaimed, his heart pounding so hard it might leap out of his chest. The queen smiled and turned, leaving the room while Tre shook like a leaf in the wind.

Skylin had been gone two days, and Tre was becoming worried. She had not told anyone where she was going, and apparently Cerra and Koda had gone with her. Tre had rode up the mountain side trail and found no sign of the big cat or the large owl. He stood by the corral and thought about his mother's comment regarding a betrothal for the twins. Her words still filled him with terror. It was possible the queen had told Skylin and in panic she had run away. That would explain her absence. As Tre stood musing by the fence, Wind suddenly appeared, racing down the path that led to the corral. Skylin's hair flew wildly about her head, and the gray stallion was lathered in sweat from running hard. As Skylin pulled the panting horse to a stop, she looked at Tre with fear-filled eyes.

Chapter 18

Tre grabbed Wind's reins as Skylin slid from the horse's back, ready to collapse. She held Tre's arm and breathlessly uttered, "Rin is in trouble." She stumbled forward to lean on the corral as Tre led Wind to a bucket of water. When the exhausted horse finished drinking, Tre placed a blanket over his back so the sweat-soaked horse didn't cool off to fast. Tre practically carried Skylin into the castle; his firm grip around her waist was all that kept her on her feet. He lowered his twin into a chair in front of the stone fireplace, hurried to the cooking room, and filled a large mug with water. He sat beside his sister and held the mug while she drank. Finally Skylin's breathing slowed. She leaned back in the chair and closed her eyes.

"Where have you been, and why is Rin in trouble?" Tre questioned his exhausted sister. He was concerned for Rin and had to find out what Skylin had seen that had her panicked like this.

Skylin opened her eyes, took a large breath, and then began. "I followed Koda out of the valley and over the mountain to the river. The same way we went when we rescued Moon. I made camp where the hills drop down to the flat land. This morning Cerra woke me growling, and Koda left his perch and started circling overhead. In the distance I could see what looked like a large dust cloud, but on the ground. I was puzzled, so I ran down to the flat land and hid behind some rocks to see what was making the huge cloud of dust." Skylin paused, her mind still not believing what she saw. "There must have been one hundred warriors dressed like the lowlanders armed with knives and spears. Wolves much bigger than the ones the lowlanders had are with the warriors. I counted at least twenty large wolves, but it was hard to see with all the dust from the desert floor. Those blackbirds are back, I saw three of them. Behind the warriors are horses pulling something, not carts like ours, but on poles dragging in the dirt. But that isn't the worst," Skylin admitted and held Tre's hands in her shaking ones. "The leader is a huge painted warrior with black braids hanging to his waist, and he rides a monstrous brown bear. He carries a huge spear with black feathers hanging from it. He is The Rider the old woman threatened Rin about." Skylin trembled and said, "He is coming and should be at the river's edge by tonight. I had to hold Cerra back or he would have been killed by the wolf pack. Tre, there are so many of them. Rin and the villagers don't stand a chance." Skylin collapsed back in the chair, too worn out to continue.

Tre was having a hard time understanding everything Skylin had told him. The threat to Rin and the villagers was real, and from Skylin's count of warriors, there would be no way the few villagers could hold off an attack of this size. Tre had to let Queen Laurel and Mallrok know that The Rider of Upland was coming and would bring destruction with him. What about Fairland, now that the road had been opened—would they be safe? Tre left Skylin resting by the fireplace and hurried to alert his mother and Mallrok. Blane must be told of the coming danger as well and ready Fairland's army. But Tre's biggest fear was for Rin,

Moon, and the new village. Was this attack the result of his decision to show pity on the few remaining lowlanders, or, in time, would The Rider of Upland have come to try once again to take Fairland as his own anyway?

Tre found his mother and Mallrok in the large banquet room looking at the colored stones Haaman had sent to the queen. Tre rushed in and quickly told them about Skylin's trip to the desert and seeing The Rider and the warriors coming toward them. When Tre finished relaying Skylin's warning, Mallrok left the castle to send for Blane and the army leaders. Queen Laurel followed Tre to the large fireplace where Old Nanny was fussing over Skylin, making sure she ate every bite of her dinner. Color had returned to his sister's face after eating the large meal, and she was looking calmer. As they waited around the roaring fireplace for Mallrok to return, the warmth from the flames helped ease the chill that had invaded the castle since Skylin's return.

"In the morning I have to ride to the bakery and warn Rin. I don't know how the villagers can hold off an attack this huge," Tre said, breaking the silence in the room.

Skylin sat up in her chair and said, "I'm coming with you." Tre knew it would be useless to argue with her, and by the look on her face her mind was made up. Her earlier fear was now gone, replaced by a resolve to never back down when threatened.

*   *   *

It was early light when Tre and Skylin tied the horses to the post in front of the bakery. They had left the castle at first light and rode hard to reach the village. They hurried into the bakery and saw Rin, Dellis, and Axe seated at one of the large tables. From the look on the Tre's face, Rin could tell something was amiss. She stood up and asked, "Tre what's wrong?"

Tre hurried over and took Rin's hand and said, "Sit down and I'll let Skylin tell you." Rin gripped Tre's hand and slowly sat, knowing it would not be good news.

Skylin quickly told Rin of her trip to the desert and seeing the warriors and the wolf pack. She finished with, "The Rider of Upland should have reached the mountain trail by now."

When Skylin described The Rider, Rin's face turned white, knowing the threat to the villagers was more serious that she imagined. She looked at Tre and stammered, "What should we do? I thought we were safe here." Her words slipped out in fear of the coming horror.

Tre didn't know how to answer his mother. He looked out the window and saw someone riding hard toward the village and shouting. Dellis rushed to the door. "That's the guard from the bridge." He went outside to meet the guard, and the others crowded behind him.

"They're here! They're here! I saw men sneaking in the trees across the river," the guard yelled as he reached the bakery. Then he turned his horse and rode back toward the fallen-tree bridge.

Dellis yelled, "Get your weapons! We can't let them cross the bridge." He grabbed a large spear, modified with a pointed metal end, and ran for his horse. Skylin raced from the bakery and jumped on Wind. She galloped up beside Dellis, and the two rode toward the bridge. Tre had not brought his staff or knife in his haste to reach Rin and looked around for something to fight with. Rin tossed a large knife to him, which he caught and shoved in his belt. Then he jumped on Pat's back, riding hard after Dellis and Skylin.

Tre halted Pat behind a rocky ledge where Wind and the two other horses stood. He quickly climbed to the bridge and saw Dellis, Skylin, and the guard crouched behind a tree. He crept over and whispered, "Can you see them?"

"Yes. They are hiding in the trees and must be waiting for someone before they cross," the guard answered.

"I'm going to crawl around the ledge and see if I can tell what they are doing," Tre said as he backed away. The high, rocky ledge extended out over the deep gorge, and when Tre reached the edge, he could hear the rushing river below him. From this height he could not see the river, only the watery mist foaming upward. His speculation about the old woman being a mystic was confirmed when he watched three blackbirds fly in. As they landed, they changed into the old woman and the two boys. These were the shape-changers that Mallrok had told him about. Tre had never seen anything like it before. The old woman's magic must be strong to be able to change into a bird. Tre knew the warriors were waiting for their mystic to arrive and backed off the ledge to warn the others.

Tre crawled back to where Dellis, Skylin, and the guard hid and told them about the old woman changing from a bird. Skylin said, "I knew she was hiding something." As they watched, about twenty warriors crept from the trees toward the bridge.

"I wish Cary was here with his bow and arrows. He could pick them off one by one as they cross the bridge," Dellis whispered.

"Then we'll have to greet them one by one when they step off the bridge," Skylin whispered back and pulled her knife. Tre wished he had brought his staff, he could fight with it better than the large knife. The magical powers of the staffs only awoke when the twins were threatened by other mystics, but the tall staff would be an excellent weapon to knock the warriors off the slippery tree bridge.

One of the warriors reached the bridge and felt the slick surface with his hands. He grunted loudly and motioned to the warriors, and one by one they started across, careful not to lose their balance and fall into deep, misty gorge. Tre had not heard Rin, Axe, and the butcher creep up behind him. When the first warrior was halfway across, Rin stepped out from behind a tree and yelled in words the warriors understood, "Come any further and you will die." She carried Windel's old sword; it was polished and sharpened and glinted in the light.

The lead warrior answered back in words Rin understood. He was Tulac's son, and she recognized him from the painted markings on his face. He had grown into a fierce-looking warrior in the likeness of his evil father. He raised his spear and pointed at Rin, and yelled more words taunting her.

Rin's face turned red with anger. She raised Windel's sword and yelled back, not bothering to speak his language, "The only way you will get Moon is over my dead body."

The warriors began to hurry across the bridge to allow the ones waiting to start crossing. Tre counted twenty armed warriors ready for battle. Dellis and Tre rushed to the bridge. Dellis knocked a spear from a warrior, and as the warrior pulled a knife on Dellis, Tre knocked him to the ground, unconscious. As more warriors made it across, the fighting intensified, and the small group of villagers was outnumbered three to one. Tre glanced up to see one of the warriors slip on the bridge and plunge into the deep gorge, too shocked to scream as he fell to his death. Tre was grateful there would be one less warrior to fight. The warriors did not expect the fighting skills of the villagers; the butcher and guard each fought two warriors. Dellis had made it a priority for all the men to keep up their daily practice, even through planting and harvesting. Rin, swinging Windel's large sword, had wounded two warriors, and they lay on the ground bleeding. Axe picked up two of the smaller warriors and threw them off the side of the mountain into the gorge, no weapon needed.

Skylin had a warrior backed into a tree who was trying desperately to escape. No worry there, Tre decided, so he ran to help the butcher fight the two warriors, each trying to cut him with a knife. Rin was swinging Windel's large sword, causing a warrior to retreat backward, when a loud war cry filled the air. Rin looked around to see Tulac's son behind her with his arm drawn back ready to plunge his spear into her back. She had no time to turn and defend herself, and the sneering look on the warrior's face said he would relish this kill. The next scream didn't come from the warrior, but from Axe, as he ran full speed into Tulac's son. He lifted the startled warrior in his large arms and charged for the mountain's edge. Axe didn't stop running as he followed the stunned warrior over the side of the mountain. Axe's guttural scream was joined by the high-pitched scream of Tulac's son echoing up from the deep gorge. It happened so fast Rin didn't have time to react but stood in shock, thinking her life had ended with the throw of the warrior's spear.

Watching their leader plunge to his death, the few remaining warriors tried to escape across the bridge, but none did. Rin rushed to the edge where Axe had disappeared and Tre had to grab hold of her arm to keep her from plunging after him. Over and over, Rin's screams of "Axe" filled the air in disbelief that Axe had vanished into the watery mist below. Tre's ears rang from Rin's screaming and Skylin ran over and placed her arms around Rin's trembling body, holding her tight, trying to bring her comfort. Dellis and the butcher began dragging the dead warriors and tossing them into the deep gorge to join the other warriors in a watery grave.

As Tre stepped back from the edge of the gorge, he saw Koda circling overhead and he yelled at the large owl pointing to the fallen-tree bridge, "Throw it into river." Koda circled downward until his large talons grabbed hold of the tree and flapping his mighty wings, he lifted the tree into the air and dropped it. Crashing sounds echoed up from the gorge, finally stopping when the tree hit the river bank.

"Look," Skylin screamed and pointed to the other side of the gorge. The old woman and two boys stood in the clearing watching and not believing what had just happened to the warrior scouts. The old woman looked deranged as she shook her fist and screamed more vile threats at Rin. Then she swiftly spun around creating a smoky mist and changed into a black bird and the two boys were changed into smaller birds. Koda screeched a warning that Tre understood. The old woman and the two boys were The Rider's messengers and must be stopped before they could report back what had happened to the scouts. Tre looked up at the large owl circling overhead and ordered, "Koda stop them." Koda's answering screech echoed back as he chased after the three messenger birds, disappearing over the mountain.

Chapter 19

It was a slow, sad walk back to the village, as everyone thought about Axe, remembering the cheerful giant of a man who would do anything for anyone. His whistled songs, which Rin had taught him, kept the villagers encouraged while working the long hours it took to rebuild their lives. He had unselfishly given his life to save Rin's. He never hesitated once he plowed into Tulac's son. His large feet never faltered as they carried him and the evil warrior over the mountain's edge. Rin stumbled along, being held upright between Tre and Dellis. When they reached the village, everyone was gathered at the bakery waiting for news. There was relief that the warriors had been defeated and the tree bridge destroyed, but also grief for the loss of a great friend. Axe held a special place in everyone's hearts.

Moon helped Tre get Rin upstairs to her room above the bakery. Rin was so distraught that she started shaking all over when she reached her bed. Moon covered her with blankets and told Tre, "I'll stay with her if you need to go."

"I must find Dellis; I want to make sure there are plans to protect the village." Tre looked down at his mother, sharing the same sadness that engulfed Rin.

Dellis and Skylin were seated at the back table when Tre came downstairs. He sat down with them. "How is Rin?" Skylin asked him from across the table.

"She is beside herself with grief. Moon is with her now." Tre looked at his sister and said, "I'm going to stay the night, but you need to go back and let mother and Mallrok know what happened. I don't think removing the bridge will stop The Rider for long. He didn't come this far to turn back at the loss of a few warriors." Tre paused a moment, then asked Skylin, "Have you seen Koda?"

Skylin shook her head no; she had not seen the large owl since he flew after the three messenger birds that morning. Skylin stood up, saying she must leave to reach Fairland before dark. Dellis walked with her outside and held Wind's reins while Skylin jumped on the horse's back. "Be careful," Dellis said as he handed her the reins and watched the dust trails created as Wind galloped away.

All the next day Rin sat in a chair and stared out the upstairs window, not uttering a word. Neither Moon nor Tre could get her to come downstairs and eat. What food they brought to her was left untouched. "I'm worried about mother," Tre told Moon. They were standing on the bakery porch looking across the long meadow. Then he admitted, "I've never seen her like this before."

Moon quietly replied, "She was very fond of Axe. They shared a special kinship. Rin is strong. She just needs time."

Dellis walked up to the bakery; he had been meeting with the village men. "Everyone is on high alert, and every day someone will watch the area where the bridge was in case they come looking for the warriors." He told Tre, and then added, "That is how the lowlanders got past Little Flock. A few raiders climbed up the steep mountain side from behind and set fire to the village."

Tre replied, "That was what they tried to do yesterday." Recalling yesterday's battle, Tre remembered he still had not seen Koda and stepped off the porch to look around. There was no sign of the large bird.

The following morning Moon was busy baking the day's bread when Rin slowly came down the stairs. Moon wiped her hands on her apron and walked over to meet Rin. She knew no words to ease Rin's grief for Axe, so she hugged her tightly, letting all of her love and care flow from her slender arms. Rin had become like a mother to Moon after she lost her own mother years ago. Tre's face brightened when Rin came into large eating room, and he hurried over and gave her a warm hug. Rin looked up at her son and asked, "Has there been any further attempts on the village?"

Tre led Rin to a table, helped her sit down, and replied, "No one has seen any signs, and Dellis has guards watching the area where the bridge was."

"I should go help Moon with the baking," Rin said and started to get up.

"Moon is very capable and has everything covered. The butcher's wife is helping with the meals." Rin smiled at hearing praise for her petite helper from Tre.

With Rin downstairs and becoming more like herself; Tre decided he would ride to Fairland after the midday meal. There were a number of things he needed to check on. Had Skylin seen Koda? Had Mallrok and Blane made plans to defend Fairland? Did The Rider know about Fairland and was the large number of warriors and wolves to fight once again to claim the hidden kingdom? Tre decided to tell Rin his plan and had just walked back into the bakery after checking on Pat when Wind skidded to a stop in front of the bakery, creating a swirl of dust.

Skylin dropped Wind's reins, slammed open the door, and franticly looked for her brother. Tre stepped out of the back, with Rin behind him, and met Skylin in the middle of the large room. "Get Dellis," she breathlessly said at the same time as Dellis rushed into the bakery. When he saw Skylin ride into the village like some monster was chasing her, Dellis dropped what he was working on and ran fast.

Skylin faced Tre and said, "When I left Fairland this morning and rode down toward the meadow, Cerra started growling and acting restless. I could tell something was upsetting him, so I rode over toward the river, and from the crest I could see the Uplanders at the place where the river raft was tied. What they were pulling behind the horses were long boats and the warriors have paddled across the river and brought the raft back." Skylin paused to catch her breath.

Dellis was stunned and exclaimed, "I forgot about the raft crossing. It's hard to find where the river curves and you can't see it unless you know where it is. How did The Rider know about it?" he puzzled.

Rin answered, "That old woman I let stay in the village. She told them about the tree bridge and the raft crossing. This is all my fault."

Skylin looked at Tre and continued, "The Rider is using the raft to cross the river, astride the back of that gigantic bear and the boats are pulling the raft across. It won't take long for all of the warriors to get across. The wolves are swimming to the other side." Skylin looked around then said, "They will be heading for the village before nightfall."

Tre had to know and asked Skylin, "Did you see the old woman or the blackbirds?"

Skylin thought for a moment then replied, "No, they weren't there."

Rin grimaced, "While we were fighting the raiding party at the tree bridge, The Rider was coming across the river. We have been tricked again."

"How can we fight all the warriors with less than twenty men?" Dellis worried aloud.

"We need a diversion. A few tricks of our own," Tre answered, and everyone looked at him, waiting for an explanation.

"They have to climb the steep path leading to the meadow; it's the only way in. We need to block the path." Tre looked around at the others.

Rin asked, "Do we have time to carry the trees that have been cut down for the new barn? Maybe we can roll the logs down and block the path and set them on fire. Those wolves won't come near a fire."

Dellis said, "I can get the men to start carrying the logs. But once they finish burning, the warriors will be able to get through."

Rin looked at Tre with pleading in her eyes. "It should give us enough time to get everyone to Fairland," Tre answered his mother's unspoken question.

Rin looked at Skylin and asked, "Will you take Moon and the other women and children to Fairland and let Queen Laurel know that, once again, we need her help?" Skylin looked like she wanted to argue with Rin; she didn't want to run from the coming fight. "Please," Rin begged and took hold of Skylin's hand, "They will be safe with you and Cerra." The look in Rin's eyes was one of anguish and distress.

Skylin gave in to Rin's request and said, "Let's get moving."

Rin shouted to Dellis as he left the bakery, "Release all the animals and drive them into the mountains. Maybe we can save them." Rin straightened her shoulders and took a deep breath, reminding Tre of what she always did before she tackled a large job. This time he was afraid the task of defeating The Rider of Upland was too large for all of them.

Dellis and the village men had started on their last trip carrying the logs to block the narrow path from the river. Skylin stood ready to leave with Moon and the women and children. The smaller children were sitting on Wind and another horse's back; they would not be able to keep up with the fast pace required to reach Fairland. Cerra paced at the edge of the village, sensing the pending danger. Tre hurried over to the frightened group of women and children to make sure everyone understood the urgency to reach Fairland before nightfall, when Koda flew in screeching loudly. One of Koda's wings looked bent, and he was flying slower than normal. Tre was sure there were some feathers missing from his large body. Skylin looked toward the large owl and said, "The Rider has crossed the river and is headed this way." Her uncanny way with Koda and Cerra still amazed him.

"What about the old woman?" Tre asked as Koda settled in a nearby tree. Koda looked at the twins, and Tre was sure the big owl smiled. Skylin grinned and exclaimed, "The evil old woman bird-changer won't be coming around ever again."

"What about the two boys?" Tre had to know the threat from The Rider's messengers was final over.

Skylin looked at Koda and interpreted, "The old woman's powers were weakened in bird form, which was why she tried to get away. Koda caught her before she could change back. When he killed her, the two boys had no powers of their own, changed back, and fell to the ground." Skylin wished she had seen the battle between Koda and the evil mystic of The Rider, sensing it had been a battle to behold.

"They're all dead?" Tre gasped in relief that both the mystic and boys were no longer a threat.

"Apparently they didn't bounce," Skylin verified Tre's question then she took hold of Wind's reins and started toward Fairland.

*   *   *

The villagers waited, hidden near the top of the narrow path that led from the river. The logs they had rolled down the path made it impassible. Cary was ready with his bow and arrows. First he would shoot fire arrows into the logs, and then he would shoot arrows into any warrior who made it through the fire. Everyone knew when the logs burnt down, the warriors would come rushing. They were only trying to slow The Rider long enough to give Skylin time to reach Fairland with the women and children. When the logs were in full blaze, the villagers would sneak away and take the high narrow trail to Fairland. By staying away from the village and the wide path that connected to the road into Fairland, they were hoping The Rider and his warriors would follow after them and not raid and pillage the new village. Tre was worried that Fairland would not be prepared, and Mallrok and Blane had not taken the threat from The Rider seriously.

Tre smelled them before he saw them approach. It was the stench like rotting flesh that signaled the arrival of The Rider and his warriors. Dellis whispered, "Cary, get the fire arrows ready." When the first fiercely painted face appeared on the narrow path, Cary shot the first fire arrow at the logs. He continued shooting arrows as fast as they were lighted, and the logs quickly burst in flames. Cries of frustration could be heard from the warriors trying to climb the steep path. Other warriors ran to the sides to avoid the flames, but the path was too narrow for them to get through. The screaming warriors ran up the path as far as they could and began throwing their spears at the unseen villagers.

As spears rained down, Tre yelled, "Let's get out of here!" As the villagers turned to leave, one of the spears found a target, and Moon's father was hit. He screamed out in pain as Dellis pulled a wooden spear from his shoulder.

"Get me something to stop the bleeding," Rin shouted as they carried the wounded man back to safety and laid him on the ground. Dellis pulled his shirt over his head, tore it into strips, and handed them to Rin. Moon's father was losing consciousness fast as his blood stained the ground red.

Tre led Pat to where Moon's father lay bleeding and told Dellis, "Help me lift him on Pat's back. Mother, you ride behind him and get to Fairland as fast as possible. Have Old Nanny tend to his wound." Tre knew Moon would be distraught if anything happened to her father. With the unconscious man held securely between her arms, Rin galloped for Fairland.

The village men raced down the high trail that led to the small stream where Tre had first begun his journey. There were not worried about leaving footprints for The Rider to follow and were hoping that he would follow them and not find the new village. Tre stopped and looked back at the plowed fields. Dellis and Cary stopped beside him. "What would happen if we burn the fields? The smoke might hide the village from The Rider."

"The crops are all harvested, and we have no use for the stubble. It might create enough smoke to keep the warriors away." Dellis looked at the fields and then said, "Cary, light your arrows." As they ran, Tre and Dellis helped Cary light arrows, and the dry stubble quickly caught fire, filling the large meadow with smoke.

The sun was dropping behind the mountains when Tre, Dellis, and the village men climbed onto the road that led to Fairland. They had run most of the way and were exhausted. Tre turned and looked back at the long meadow filled with smoke. It was hard to see anything in the billowing fire as the stubble burnt slowly to the ground. Tre wondered if it would be enough to detour The Rider away from the village. One of the men called out and pointed up the road, "Riders are coming."

Blane rode up, leading a small band of army men. He jumped off his horse and said, "We've come to make sure you get to Fairland safely. Skylin was worried and sent horses." Tre was grateful to see Pat and Wind, and he patted Pat's strong neck before jumping onto his back. The big red horse didn't look tired from carrying Rin and Moon's father to Fairland. Blane handed Dellis the reins to Wind and told him, "Skylin said to tell you not to fall off."

"That sounds like her," Dellis replied as he jumped on the trim gray stallion.

"What plans have been made to defend Fairland?" Tre asked Blane. The army leader told him lookouts have been posted to report the progress of The Rider, and Queen Laurel sent out orders for everyone to get to the castle. We want to try to stop as many warriors as possible before they make it to town and will defend the road from both sides. We should be able to protect the castle since it's built against the mountain. Tre agreed; it sounded like the best solution to keep the approaching warriors out of Fairland. Tre turned to Dellis. "I need to find Mallrok and I'll see you later at the castle." Then he swiftly rode toward Fairland.

Mallrok was in the large meeting room, and when Tre entered, he turned and said, "The queen just left to check with Veerna and make sure there is enough food to feed everyone."

Tre replied, "I need to talk to you and see what you can tell me about the old ones and where the Uplanders and The Rider come from. We need to find some way to defeat them. There are so many warriors and wolves; I'm concerned Blane and the army won't be able to hold them off."

Mallrok shook his gray head and sat down with a far-off look on his face. He finally said, "Many years ago the ancients battled a fierce people with dark magic. They came from beyond the desert and made their homes in high cliffs above the flat land. They had magic so powerful that our old ones could not defeat them. The lowlanders you fought were descendants of them. I know little else that was passed down, and the only way to protect Fairland was to seal it off from the outside."

Tre told Mallrok, "I think The Rider has these same dark powers. He has a large pack of wolves twice the size that the lowlanders had, and there was a mystic with him that could change into a bird and brought him messages."

"Yes, Skylin told me. I fear for Fairland." Mallrok slowly shook his head.

"Do you know of any way to defeat him or how we can stop his powers?" Tre was desperate for any help or knowledge. Mallrok looked at Tre and had no answer.

*   *   *

The following day, everyone in Fairland had made it to the castle. They brought vegetables and grain from the barns to help feed the large number of people. The corral was full of horses and a few cows for milking. Any man that was able to hold a weapon, Blane put on guard around the castle, leaving the army free to defend the road. Word had reached Queen Laurel that scouts had been spotted near the road and The

Rider with his warriors and wolves would be close behind. Blane left the castle that morning to station the Fairland army along the road to stop the Uplanders from entering Fairland. The brave men of Fairland were outnumbered, but they would stand strong against the coming menace.

Skylin stomped into the room and told Tre, "The fighting has started. I can't believe mother won't let us join the fight." Her irritation was evident at having to stay inside the castle, and Tre knew she was worried about Dellis. He and the village men had joined with the Fairland army to defend the road.

"She has her reasons, and Mallrok said this battle isn't ours." Tre tried to reason with her. Tre knew Mallrok was worried about The Rider's dark magic and he was concerned for Queen Laurel and the twins. Skylin paced back and forth in front of the large fireplace. Waiting was hard for Tre, so he could only imagine the stress she was feeling. Tre looked out the large window. The sun was about to drop behind the mountain, and darkness would soon replace the light.

Tre could feel the rumble of feet before he looked out and saw the men running down the road that led to the castle. Many of them carried wounded men between them and everyone looked like they had been injured to some degree. Tre could tell the battle had not gone well for Fairland, and he raced outside to help with the injured. Old Nanny had cleared out the large meeting room and filled it with mats and blankets; she was ready to tend to the wounded. Water and rolled bandages were stored against the wall where a group of townswomen waited. As the wounded men were carried in, the women rushed to them.

After the last man entered the castle grounds, Blane ordered, "Bar the gate." Blood flowed from a large gash in his arm. Tre rushed to the army leader and helped him inside. "There were too many of them, and they just kept coming. When The Rider came down the road surrounded by those huge wolves, I gave the order to retreat. We just couldn't hold them off any longer." Blane collapsed against Tre.

*   *   *

It was a long night, and the lit torches around the castle cast an eerie light outside the windows. Tre could hear movements from outside the castle walls, but in the darkness he could not see anything. He knew the castle was surrounded by warriors, and the constant howling from the large wolves filled the air, frightening the women and children. Finally the darkness began to fade as morning approached.

A tired Queen Laurel stood looking out the large castle window when she placed a hand on her chest and gasped. Tre, Skylin, and Mallrok hurried to her side and saw The Rider astride the enormous bear. Up close the bear's long brown hair was dirty and matted. The bear opened his huge jaw and growled, exposing large yellowed teeth. The loud growl echoed throughout the castle, causing everyone to rush to a window. Terror filled the people when they saw the huge bear and vicious wolf pack.

The Rider raised his long black spear in the air and yelled. Rin pushed her way beside Tre and looked out the window at The Rider. The Rider yelled again, violently shaking his long black spear. "He is calling for surrender of the castle," Rin interpreted. One of the large wolves jumped against the locked gate, causing it to shake violently. It would only take a few more impacts and the gate would give way allowing the warriors to enter. Tre knew that to surrender the castle would mean certain death for everyone. The Rider would take no prisoners.

Tre did not see Mallrok leave the queen's side and was shocked when the tall, white-robed figure walked out of the castle door toward the gate. Mallrok, holding his staff in his hand, stopped and yelled at The Rider, "You have no right to be here. Leave now. Your dark powers will not prevail."

The Rider raised up high on the bear's back and menacingly laughed at Mallrok. Then he threw the black feather-covered spear he held directly at Mallrok. It landed upright and stuck in the ground in front of Mallrok. The spear began to tremble, sparks flew from it, and then the spear changed into a large, hissing, black serpent. The serpent grew as tall as Mallrok and its large head leaned back, revealing huge fangs dripping with slime. As the serpent lunged at him, Mallrok raised his staff to defend himself, but the black serpent knocked the staff aside.

Tre saw Skylin race from the room grabbing Rin's large sword as she ran, and he hurried after her. They reached the castle door in time to see the tall black serpent bite Mallrok in the neck, sinking its slimy fangs in deep.

"NO!" Skylin screamed and ran to Mallrok as he vainly tried to pull the serpent away from his neck. Skylin raised the large sword and brought it down, cutting the serpent in half. The head of the serpent released its hold on Mallrok's neck and dropped to the ground beside its other half. Tre caught Mallrok in his arms as the old mystic collapsed. Skylin stepped back from the two slimy halves and stood beside Tre. Together they watched in shock as each half turned into a complete serpent and both slithered back to The Rider. The Rider reached down and grabbed the two black serpents. He held them up high, laughing menacingly.

Then one of the serpents swallowed the other's tail and they changed back into the large black spear. The Rider's vile laughter followed the twins as they carried Mallrok back into the castle.

Chapter 20

Old Nanny demanded the unconscious Mallrok be carried to the book room and not to the large meeting room with the other injured men. She muttered to herself, "The dark magic . . . The dark magic," and shuffled to the cooking room. From a hidden place in the large pantry she removed an old clay pot with a sealed lid. She carefully carried the pot to the book room and shut the door. She sat the old pot on the table and pulled away the binding that sealed it. From her pocket she took a small container of purple liquid and slowly poured it into the pot. Puffs of colored smoke rose as old nanny stirred in the liquid. When the smoke ebbed away she carried the pot to Mallrok, whispering to him, "hurry and drink the potion." Mallrok's gray head leaned to one side, and Old Nanny had to hold his head steady as, sip by sip, he slowly drank the purple liquid. When the pot was empty, Old Nanny stood back and watched Mallrok. After a few minutes, she backed out of the room, closing the door behind her.

Tre was in the large meeting room checking on the injured men and saw Blane with his arm bandaged, leaning against the wall talking to Dellis. Dellis turned when Tre approached, and Tre noticed a large gash down the side of his friend's face. Tre asked Dellis what happened, and Dellis replied, "It's not deep and probably won't even leave a scar.

If it does, Skylin said it would improve my looks." Dellis' smile was lopsided. Tre knew Dellis would have one big scar when his wound healed.

Tre turned to Blane and asked, "How many men have we lost?"

"Only a few. Old Nanny saved most of the injured, but it will take time for some of them to heal," Blane said as he sadly looked across the room at the injured men.

Dellis held Tre's arm. "Did you hear Moon's father didn't make it; he lost too much blood for Old Nanny to save him."

Tre was stunned. He had not thought about Moon's father since arriving at the castle. He knew Moon would be crushed at losing her only parent, and she had been very close to her father. "Where is she?" he asked Dellis.

"Helping Rin with the food," Dellis told him.

Tre walked into the cooking room and saw Rin stirring a large pot. "Where is Moon?" he asked her.

"I'm here," a soft reply came from the pantry. Moon was carrying a tray of food, and Tre walked over and took the tray from her, placing it on the table.

He held her hands and said, "I just heard about your father. I'm so sorry."

Moon's lower lip trembled as she tried not to shed further tears. "He died defending Rinland, and I am very proud of him." Tre looked in her large brown eyes filled with sorrow. Moon was small, but her strength was large.

*   *   *

Queen Laurel sent word to Blane asking that he and the army leaders meet her by the fireplace because the large meeting room was filled with mats of injured men. When

Blane and the men were gathered around she told them, "We must defend the castle at all costs. We cannot allow those warriors to enter." Then she asked, "How many men are still able to fight?"

Blane reported, "A few men have been killed and some badly injured, but most of the men are still able to fight."

"The Rider will not wait long and has his warriors positioned around the castle. In the morning I am certain he will attack," the queen told Blane.

"No one has seen The Rider since this morning, and with no guards posted outside the castle wall, we don't know what he is doing," Blane explained.

"Make sure the torches stay lighted all night," the queen ordered and stood to leave the room when Koda flew down and landed on the back balcony wall. The queen looked toward Koda and he issued a quiet screech, and the queen nodded her head. Then Koda flew away.

Tre paced around the castle, at a loss of what to do. He knew time was running out for Fairland, and The Rider would soon return. He went to the library to try to solve the riddle of the serpent. He knew the answer was in the ancient scripts. The serpent was real, and the dark magic still alive. The old ones knew that one day the serpent would return to claim farland. He slowly opened the door to the library, not wanting to disturb Mallrok and was surprised to find the room empty. Old Nanny must have moved Mallrok to the meeting room with the other injured men. He closed the door and picked up the old book and sat down. He had read the riddle of the serpent at least a hundred times and had still no clue of the missing words to finish the last line and defeat the serpent. For good to win over evil, they had to cast down something, but what? He wished Mallrok was here so he could ask him.

The door slowly opened, and Skylin leaned in and looked around. "Where's Mallrok?" she whispered.

"I don't know. He wasn't here when I came in," Tre answered.

Skylin looked at what her brother was doing and glared at him in frustration and yelled, "Still reading those old books when there are warriors outside ready to kill everyone?"

"I'm trying to figure out how to defeat the serpent," Tre explained to his sister as she stormed off, loudly slamming the door.

Skylin found Queen Laurel and Old Nanny in the cooking room talking with Rin. She interrupted them. "Where is Mallrok?" The three women stopped talking and turned to look at her, but no one answered. "Is he dead?" she demanded and glared at Old Nanny. Old Nanny had many years of dealing with Skylin's glares, and she turned her back on Skylin's outrage. "Mother," Skylin now pleaded.

"He's fine," the queen told her and then turned to Rin, asking how long the food rations would last. Skylin whirled around and stomped from the room, upset because no one would tell her anything.

The castle guards kept the torches lit again that night. The constant howling by the wolves kept everyone on edge and unable to sleep. All during the night warriors would sneak up and throw spears at the guards as they restlessly waited for The Rider's signal to attack the castle. During the long night, everyone's mind repeated the question, "Was this the end of Fairland?"

*   *   *

The morning light was welcomed and dreaded by Tre. He was glad the night, filled with long, tense hours of waiting, was over, but dawn would bring The Rider with his warriors and wolves, and the battle for Fairland would begin. Tre knew there were not enough men to keep the warriors out of the castle for long, and there were the vicious wolves to contend with. How would The Rider use his dark magic? Tre still had no answer to the riddle of how to kill the serpent. If The Rider's dark powers were defeated it would end the battle. The ancients knew this to be true.

The escalating noise from outside the castle walls signaled The Rider had returned. The warriors started loudly chanting, running around, and shaking their spears. The wolves became more agitated, and their howling increased. Tre stood up straight, squared his shoulders, and took a deep breath. Elsewhere Rin did the same, though he was not aware of it. The old knife the butcher had given him was pushed inside his belt. Tre reached for his staff and walked to the large castle doors. Blane and Dellis were waiting there, and both carried weapons, prepared to fight, although both were injured. Tre pulled opened the large wooden doors and saw The Rider astride the bear. The huge brown bear was as wide as the gate, and its bulk would overpower the gate when The Rider signaled to attack.

Rin stepped outside carrying Windel's sword. Tre turned to his mother and asked, "Please go back and help guard Queen Laurel and the women. If we can't stop the warriors, get everyone in the meeting room and block the doors." Tre knew The Rider would take no prisoners, but Rin, Queen Laurel, and Moon would be safe for as long as possible. At the pleading look in Tre's eyes, Rin left to go to find Queen Laurel and Moon.

The Rider sat on the back of the giant brown bear, glaring down at the small group of men standing in front of the castle door. He laughed and pointed his spear when

Skylin stepped out with her staff in one hand and her knife in the other, ready for the coming fight. Tre knew The Rider was taunting Skylin because she had tried to kill the serpent when it attacked Mallrok. *Where was Mallrok?* Tre wondered. He had not seen him since he carried the unconscious mystic into the library yesterday morning. Then Tre heard Mallrok tell him, "This is not my fight." Tre's heart stop as his mind replayed the words only he heard, *This is not my fight.* Tre knew that Mallrok could not help them. The Rider started chanting and swinging the large spear in circles above his head, and black feathers started flying around him as they came loose. The warriors and the wolves broke into a frenzied rage as The Rider chanted louder encased in a black whirlwind of feathers. Tre felt a chill run down his back at the horrifying scene and knew the few Fairland brave could not defeat this menace.

A loud ear piercing yelp from one of the wolves quieted the clamor. It sounded as if the wolf had been gravely injured. Tre could not see beyond the castle wall and wondered what was happening. Then another wolf yelped out loud in pain. The Rider stopped his chanting and turned to see what was going on when one of the wolves behind the huge bear violently yelped and leaped high over the gate, landing in front of the castle door. The huge animal began shaking violently, and foam started coming from his mouth. Then the large wolfish creature began shrinking in size. The animal, now the size of a dog, stood up on its wobbly legs and growled at the men guarding the door. Suddenly a carved wood—handled knife hit the animal directly between the eyes. The wolf wobbled on its shaky legs for a moment and then dropped over dead. Skylin ran to retrieve her knife and kicked the dead wolf to the side of the path.

' Different growling sounds were heard, lower pitched than the wolves' shrill howls. From behind the corral a large pack of badger-like animals raced on sharp-clawed feet toward the smaller wolves. Tre ran to the dead wolf, reached down, and pulled out a small dart from the animal's neck. The same type of dart the slags used on the men guarding the barns. He held the dart up for Skylin and Blane to see and yelled, "We have help from the slags." With renewed energy Tre ran back to the castle door.

The Rider shrieked in alarm, watching his wolf pack being dissolved by a magic that overpowered his dark magic that created the wolf pack. One by one The Rider watched the wolves shrink to normal size. He was confused, where did this new magic come from? When the badger-like animals killed the last wolf, The Rider became enraged and screamed. He urged the large bear forward, the gate crushing beneath its bulk. Tre and Skylin rushed out, standing together to block the brown beast. They held their staffs in front, ready to fight. The Rider glared at the carving on the staffs and recognized the symbols. The bear was so close that its hot breath smelling of rotting flesh singed the air. The Rider jumped from the bear's back and stepped in front of the brown beast. With both hands he plunged his black spear into the ground directly in front of the twins.

As before, the spear began to tremble and the ground around it shook. Then it transformed once again into the large black serpent growing in height until it was as tall as the twins. Hissing, its large head revealed dripping fangs ready to strike, and its black eyes darted back and forth, watching the twins. Skylin screamed and lunged at the black menace before it could strike her brother like it did Mallrok. This time she swung her staff directly at its puffed out head. As Skylin's staff hit the serpent's head, it swiftly coiled itself around, pulling the staff from her hands. As the serpent uncoiled itself, Skylin's staff dropped harmlessly to the ground. The Rider sneered at Skylin, uttering words no one understood, and threateningly stepped toward her.

Cast down, cast down, the ancient words echoed in Tre's head. He had to do something to protect his twin from The Rider. Tre held his staff in his hands and remembered the ancient words about the power of the staff. Tre stepped forward, and, following The Rider's example, using both hands he plunged his staff into the ground directly in front of the hissing black serpent.

Tre's staff stuck upright in the ground before the black serpent, and again the ground began to tremble. The Rider screamed when the ground beneath his feet shook, and he ran behind the hissing black serpent, crowding close to the bear. White sparks shot outward from Tre's staff, and then a bolt of lightning hit the ground. A glimmering white snake, much larger than the black serpent, appeared out of the lightning bolt. Fangs dripping with slime, the black serpent struck out at the shinning white snake. Instantly the white snake moved aside and quickly coiled itself around the malevolent serpent. Slowly the white snake began to tighten its coil, squeezing tighter and tighter until the black serpent fell limp and turned back into a spear. Everyone was stunned, most of all Tre, as he watched the glowing white snake glide to his side and change back into his staff. Tre grabbed hold of his staff and ran to where the spear lay on the ground. He picked up the spear and broke it into harmless pieces of wood that he threw aside.

The Rider shrieked in anger at seeing the black serpent defeated. The huge brown bear roared out loud as it backed up the path, and, in its haste to escape, knocked The Rider to the ground. Skylin quickly picked up her staff and started swinging it at The Rider. As the cowering leader backed away from Skylin's blows, a large yellow cat leaped up beside her. Cerra had been behind the corral with Mallrok, waiting until given the order to attack. Until then, the battle had not been Cerra's either. The great cat leaped at The Rider, and with his large jaws finished what Skylin started. The Rider of Upland was as dead as his spear. Cerra stepped up on The Rider's back and loudly roared a cry of victory. Tre turned and yelled to Blane, "Now it's time to fight!" Blane motioned for the men filling the large castle hallway to follow him as he ran toward the shocked warriors.

The huge brown bear lumbered up the path to escape, his huge paws moving as fast as his bulk would allow. Koda screeched from above, flew down, and with his large talons grabbed hold of the lumbering bear, pulling large clumps of hair and skin from its back. The bear lifted his immense head and roared out in pain. Skylin shouted, "Cerra, get rid of that beast forever." The big cat jumped the castle wall and ran after the retreating bear, joining Koda in the chase.

Tre rushed over and exclaimed, "That bear is three times larger than Cerra."

Skylin looked at her brother and laughed. "It's not the size of the cat in the fight that matters, but the size of the fight in the cat." Then his twin rushed off down the path to help fight the retreating warriors. Tre stopped for a moment, realizing those words also described his sister, and then he raced after her.

*   *   *

The battle with the warriors lasted into the day. With the death of The Rider, the warriors were left without the protection of their dark master and were no longer as fierce. The battle lasted so long due to the great number of warriors, each warrior fighting to the death, not willing or understanding what it meant to surrender. This prevented Tre from once again having to decide whether to spare Fairland's enemies.

Tre was exhausted as he slowly walked back to the castle. It wasn't just today's fighting, but the combination of everything that had happened since the raiding party was spotted at the tree bridge. Blane caught up to him and reported the Fairland army suffered no more deaths, although there had been a number of brave men wounded. He told Tre the weapons Kross made from the metal the slags mined were far superior to the wooden ones of the warriors.

Tre looked up to see Mallrok and Haaman standing by the corral, and he walked over to thank them. Without help from these two mystics, Fairland would not have survived the day. He hugged Mallrok firmly, saying how thankful he was to see the tall, white-robed man. Tre turned to Haaman. "Fairland can't thank you enough. How you turned those wolves back to normal was amazing?"

Haaman bowed and said, "It was the slags fight too. We would not have survived if The Rider had conquered Fairland." Haaman bowed again and backed away into the shadow of the tall trees. Tre noticed the band of badgers waiting in the trees, but what surprised him most were the small white figures that climbed down from the trees wearing black cloths over their eyes. The slags were strange looking before, but Tre had to stop himself from laughing out loud as the small masked creatures disappeared behind Haaman into the shadows. Mallrok watched with Tre and explained, "We had to use the black cloth to allow the slags to come out in the light. Without covering their eyes, they would not have been able to see to shoot the darts."

"Amazing." Tre shook his head. "I need to check on Rin and mother." He told Mallrok and turned and walked to the castle.

That night the large castle was full of joy and of sorrow. Everyone was happy The Rider of Upland and the serpent was defeated and sad because of the many injured men and the loss of others. Queen Laurel had proclaimed the following day would be a remembrance day and, every year thereafter, a day to honor those who had fought to keep Fairland free. Tomorrow they would bury their dead and move back into their homes.

Tre found Rin in the large meeting room talking with Dellis and Skylin. They were making plans to leave for the village in the morning. The two wounded village men would be well enough to ride a horse. The rest of the men would walk with the women and children. Rin told Tre in two days they would bury Moon's father and asked if he would come. "Of course I'll be there. I need to be with the queen tomorrow, but I will ride over the following day." Skylin told Tre that she was going to accompany the villagers home, and Tre could attend the burials with Queen Laurel. Skylin planned on staying in Rinland and helping Dellis look for the animals they had chased into the mountains. Since The Rider never found the small village, all their homes should be okay.

*   *   *

A slight breeze stirred the air where Tre stood on the small hillside. He had left Pat tied by the bakery and climbed the hill to watch as Rin, Moon, and the villagers buried Moon's father. Moon held tightly to Rin's hand as she stood and watched her father's body placed in the ground. Moon scattered flowers across the grave as she whispered her good-bye. Then the villagers placed stones to mark the gravesite. Another pile of stones was nearby; it was for Axe. Rin insisted the gentle, giant man be remembered, and flowers adorned the ground around the stones. Skylin and Dellis led their horses as they walked up to stand beside Tre. They had been out looking for the cattle and other animals they had released. Tre quietly asked if they found any of the animals, and Skylin smiled and said, "Every one of them. Once the smoked died away they found their way back to the meadow." Skylin looked happier than Tre ever remembered seeing her.

Rin started singing a song Tre remembered from his childhood. Moon and the villagers joined in, and the words echoed away when the song ended. As the villagers turned to return home, Tre thought he heard the song's melody being mimicked by a bird. He looked around, but it was so faint that he must have imagined it. Then he heard it again, stronger and coming closer. He turned to where the sound was coming from. Over a nearby hill a big, burly shape appeared. The whistled melody grew louder as the shape slowly limped forward, leaning heavily against a large yellow cat. It was Axe, scratched and bloody, with one arm tied close to his chest. He stopped on top of the hill and raised his good arm in a mountain salute and gave a loud yell. The large yellow cat joined him with a ferocious growl. An earsplitting screech overhead signaled Koda's arrival. Tre had been worried about Koda and Cerra since they took off after the monstrous bear, but Skylin had not, telling Tre they were fine; she just didn't know where they were.

Tre heard his twin exclaim, "So that's where you've been, bringing Axe home."

"Axe!" Rin screamed and ran as fast as she could to him. With his good arm he caught her. Rin was laughing and crying and saying his name over and over. She put her arms around him to help him down the hill. Cerra's job was over, and he bounded toward the tall trees that lined the meadow. Tre was so absorbed in watching the reunion of Rin and Axe that he startled when a small hand slid inside his. He looked down to see Moon had come up beside him. Her soft brown eyes still glistened from tears shed for her father, and the slight breeze lifted her long hair around her slim shoulders. Tre smiled down at her and squeezed her hand, knowing it was where it belonged.

Tre looked at his twin, who was standing next to Dellis and grinning widely as she watched Rin and Axe. Tre reached out and took Sklylin's hand and raised their arms in a mountain salute and gave a victory yell and she joined him—The Twins of Fairland.